Star Spangled Homicide

A Short Paranormal Cozy Mystery

B I Skinner

Acknowledgments

For Snickers

From discarded rabbit to character in a cozy mystery.

Thank you for choosing me to foster you.

Special thanks to my incredible editor Amanda Skinner.

I hope you didn't get carpal tunnel editing all of this!

Contents

Chapter 1

Angry words echo across Snowball Park.

"How dare you!"

All eyes turn to see a fight brewing between Mayor Doyle and Sam Bunmi, the Thai One On Food Truck owner, during the Crested Peaks 4th of July Festival.

I can't believe my own eyes when Mr. Bunmi shoves Mayor Doyle into the snowcone booth, sending pointy paper cups and bottles of colored syrup flying.

The shocked snowcone vendor leaps out of the way right before Mayor Doyle throws a fistful of crushed ice at Mr. Bunmi. Festival-goers abandon their picnics and funnel cakes to gather around the fight.

"Boss, do something!" Aranya cries. Mr. Bunmi is Aranya's father, and she has worked for me at Marcall's Breakfast Cafe for about a year. The few times I've met him, he seemed so mild-mannered and soft-spoken. How is this fight happening?

"What can I do?" I respond, feeling helpless watching two grown men scuffle mere feet away. Unfortunately, the growing crowd is more interested in recording the fight on their phones than breaking it up.

"Witchcraft!" she shouts, desperately.

Until I moved back to Crested Peaks, ten years after my high school graduation, I denied I was a witch, and my skills were rusty at best. But with my best friend Miranda as my witching mentor, I'm getting pretty good at it.

But I hate that it didn't occur to me right away. I scan the area for something to stop the fight. Now they're on the ground, half wrestling, half throwing punches.

When I spot a fire hydrant several feet away, I channel my mystic energy onto the cap to remove it and open the valve. It moves. An entire inch. Talk about anti-climactic and not at all helpful.

The angry men and the crowd distract me and make it hard to focus on the kind of power I need to loosen the heavy cap. I take a deep breath and block out everything around me. The cap loosens a bit more. Why isn't it doing what I need it to do?

"Hurry, Charlotte!" Aranya begs in the background. I close my eyes, breathe deep, and ground myself, calling on the earth's energy to bolster the natural power I need to flow through me. Then I use every bit of concentration that I have, and the cap finally flies off in a loud clatter.

Water sprays from the hydrant in a colossal rush, startling the men enough to pause their vicious fight. They back off, spluttering and cursing while the frigid water hammers them so hard that Mr. Bunmi can't stand up. The stream even catches several bystanders who stop filming long enough to back out of its reach.

I'm relieved when two Crested Peaks Police Department officers elbow their way through the crowd. "Step back, please! Out of the way!" they shout.

Each one grabs at a man, pulling them apart, and the crowd groans with disappointment when the entertainment stops.

The officers haul the still squirming, shouting, sopping wet men through the crowd back to their patrol cars, where they shove each one into the cars' back seats. I watch as they question Mr. Bunmi and Mayor Doyle. Each man gestures angrily while giving their version of the event.

Now that the excitement is over, the crowd disperses and slowly returns to enjoying the festival. The gallons and gallons of water I released into the area have created a growing pond everyone is now sidestepping. The Crested Peaks Fire Department arrives to replace the cap, and they aren't happy.

I do my best to sneak away from the area before anyone realizes who unleashed the torrent of water on the fighters. I'm mad I didn't think to use witchcraft right away. Even though my magic improves daily, it's still unnatural to me at times.

I wave when I see Detective Andrew Bailey slowly making his way through the crowd. Everyone automatically steps aside for the tall, dark, and handsome detective.

His confident stride along with his emerald green eyes, short dark hair, and athletic build automatically command respect from those around him. What? Too cliche? It's the truth!

"What was that all about?" I ask him, nodding my head toward the men still detained by the police. Oh, did I mention the detective is also my boyfriend?

Did I also mention that only weeks after I returned to Crested Peaks (to inherit my Gran's breakfast cafe, Marcall's,) Detective Bailey dragged me down to the police station on suspicion of murdering my landlord?

Okay, so maybe dragged is a bit hyperbolic. I actually rode in the front seat of his squad car. And only for questioning. Even so, it was unpleasant, and I prefer not to think about it.

"Mr. Bunmi is angry because Mayor Doyle, who owns the lot where they host the Farmer's Market, raised the rent for the food trucks," he explains

"That must be a heck of a raise," I point out.

Drew nods. "Bunmi says he and several others can't afford to park at the event anymore."

"Why don't they park on the street outside the farmer's market?" I ask. "I've seen food trucks do that."

"The city council recently passed an ordinance saying they can't park on the street," Drew explains. Frustration etches across his face.

"Isn't that convenient?" I scowl. "They can't park on the street, so they have to park on the high-priced lot that the mayor owns."

"It's corrupt," Drew mutters.

"Someone should do something about that," I point out.

"Yep, but who?"

I shake my head sadly. "I don't know." City ordinances are none of my business. I just try to keep my restaurant running smoothly, which isn't always easy given the trouble that finds me. But I've sworn off all of that. From now on, I leave any criminal investigations to the CPPD and politics to the politicians.

Then Damien, my height challenged, stocky, head chef, sloshes his way through the now lake-sized pond towards us. "Why must these events always end in chaos?" he asks.

"But no murders this time, right?" I point out.

Drew and Damien groan. Last year's 4th of July Festival ended early when my rabbit familiars found the magician's assistant stabbed to death, with Damien's cousin the primary suspect. So, sue me, but I happen to think a fistfight is much better than murder.

Chapter 2

Later that evening

The town gathers eagerly for the second time today to enjoy the annual fireworks show held behind Hotel Glacier over the lake. I shudder when I recall how we found Santa's body floating there during the community Christmas party. At first, we assumed he had too many peppermint martinis, but it turned out to be something far more sinister.

Tonight, though, the talk is all about the fight at the park. Rumors range from the mayor having an affair with Mrs. Bunmi to Mr. Bunmi telling the mayor his mama wears combat boots. Neither of which is true, I'm sure.

"Charlotte! Hey Charlotte!" Serenity Clements calls out to me through the crowd. She's the new owner of Serenity's Sweets, the candy shop next door to Marcall's Breakfast Cafe. "I love what you did to your hair today!"

"Thanks!" I respond. One of the coolest things about being a witch is I can change my hair color every day if I want. Today I swirled multi-colored highlights of red, white, and blue throughout my long tresses. Even I'm impressed with the way it turned out.

I haven't known Serenity long, but I like her and often find myself seeking her advice. "Nice job breaking up the fight this afternoon," she tells me.

"Ugh." I grimace. "I'm so mad that I froze at first. Why didn't I think to use magic right away?"

"You did the right thing in the end, and that's what counts. You shouldn't be so hard on yourself. You're considered a community leader, you know," she consoles me.

I laugh so hard several people turn to see what the joke is about.

"Why are you laughing?" Serenity asks.

"I thought you were kidding," I respond, narrowing my eyes at her. She is joking, right?

"Charlotte, think about how many times you saved this community since you moved back here."

I continue to stare at her in confusion. Clearly this woman has been sampling too many enchanted peppermint sticks. "I don't know about that."

"You really don't, do you? You aren't just playing modest."

"I wouldn't say that *I* saved this community." I insist.

"What about the time you prevented a mafia takeover?" she points out.

"Eh," I wiggle my hand. "I had help with that, you know."

"You're the one who brought down that disgusting reporter and turned all the horrible news into good publicity for us," Damien reminds us, appearing at my side.

"You guys helped me with that," I remind him.

"But *you* lead the way," he insists.

"Don't forget how you discovered the international smuggling ring," my best friend Miranda, and owner of the Bean Around a Bit Coffee Shop across the street from Marcall's, joins the conversation.

"You're all embarrassing me now. I didn't do it by myself. I don't deserve all the credit."

"You could do amazing things, you know." Serenity waggles her finger at me before moving on through the crowd.

I watch her walk away, convinced she's eaten too many rum-infused chocolates this afternoon. Me. A community leader. As if!

Chapter 3

"Hey, where are the rabbits?" I ask, scanning the crowd. They rode with us to the lake for the fireworks show, but now I realize I haven't seen them since we got out of the car.

"They're at the bus station picking up Snickers," Poppy, Damien and Tom's newly adopted four-year-old foster daughter, informs me. Before she came to us, I was the only person who could communicate with the rabbits.

Weren't we surprised when we discovered she's a witch too! Even more remarkable, she can talk to *all* animals. Except their dog Bubbles who doesn't talk. The rabbits tell me they think this is unnatural. Yes, that's right. The talking rabbits think a dog who doesn't talk is unnatural. Welcome to my world.

"They're where, picking up who?" What is she talking about? Surely, she's mistaken. Why would the rabbits be at the bus station, and who is this Snickers?

"Snickers. Their cousin from Toronto." She says, as if a bus-riding rabbit cousin needs no further explanation.

"The rabbits told you this?"

"Yes."

"Why didn't the rabbits tell me?"

"They wanted to surprise you."

I'm sure they did. Marshall and Marcus invited Stumpy, the cat who lived in the Italian restaurant next door, to live with us after the restaurant owner passed away. The kicker is they did it without telling me.

Stumpy is a gray tabby cat with an extra-long tail and no back feet. He followed us out to the car one day after closing, and when I asked him why, the rabbits said he needed a new home; so, they told him he could live with us.

"Please tell me they haven't asked him to move in with us, without my permission."

"No," Poppy responds without looking up from her coloring book. Her dark brown pigtails are tied up with festive red, white, and blue ribbons. "Snickers lives in Toronto with his wife and their four kids. He's on vacation."

"Wonderful. Maybe his wife is the one who needs a vacation," I mutter. I won't ask how a rabbit got a wife. Or four kids.

Marshall and Marcus, my rabbit familiars, belonged to my Gran, who won them ages ago in a poker game. Until she died, only she could communicate with them.

They're a pair of orange and white brothers whose goal in life is to scam as many treats from unsuspecting residents and shopkeepers throughout the Crested Peaks community as they can.

After Gran died, though, their ability to communicate somehow transferred to me. As much as I complain about their mischievous ways, they have been instrumental in helping me solve the various mysteries that Crested Peaks attracts.

"Why didn't they take Stumpy with them?" I ask, pointing to him as he sits on the blanket next to her, watching her color a fish.

Stumpy can't talk to me, but he talks to the rabbits and Poppy, who translate for me. He tells us he's a war veteran, and that's how he lost his back feet. For a two-footed cat, he gets along surprisingly well.

I'm not sure about the war veteran part, but who could have imagined talking rabbits with a cousin from Canada, so I guess anything is possible?

"He didn't want to miss the fireworks," Poppy says.

Miranda reaches over me to grab a grape before popping it into her mouth. "Can you believe that fight this afternoon? I don't know Mr. Bunmi that well, but he always seems so laid back. I'm still stunned he tore into the mayor like that," she says.

"Me too! Drew said that the mayor owns the lot where they park the food trucks during the farmer's market, and he's raising the rent so high that the Bunmi's don't think they can afford it anymore," I tell her.

"Can they park on the street? Or at Snowball Park? I've seen a lot of parks trucked there."

I shake my head. "Nope. Not anymore. The mayor and city council just passed an ordinance prohibiting street parking for the food trucks."

"Can they do that? That isn't fair. Especially if it mainly benefits the mayor who owns the lot where they rent!" Miranda responds angrily.

"Seems like they're always picking on the little guy, doesn't it?"

"Hey, here come the rabbits now!" she points at the three rabbits approaching us. "The little striped guy must be the cousin."

"How can rabbits have a cousin who rides a bus from Canada?" Drew asks.

"Or rides a bus from anywhere?" I point out.

"I still can't believe any of this is possible," he says, watching them as they continue to hop our way.

"I've given up trying to explain it." I shrug.

Drew is a Non Supernatural but has always known that I'm a witch, like my parents and my grandmother. What he didn't realize at first, because I don't tell many people, is that my rabbit familiars talk to me. After too many slip-ups, I finally confessed. That was a fun conversation, trust me.

"Hey, lady," Marcus says. "This is our cousin Snickers." I don't know why they call me lady. Unfortunately, it often precedes a declaration of illegal activity they've unearthed. Thank goodness that can't be the case this time. Who would murder someone right before the fireworks show?

"This is our cousin, Snickers," he tells me.

"Hey Snickers, nice to meet you." Snickers blinks back at me, and I notice he looks nothing like his cousins. His ears stick straight up, whereas Marshall's and Marcus' ears point sideways. Like helicopters. Snickers also has a bold mixture of different colored stripes, and his fur appears plush and velvety. He's adorable.

"You didn't find any bodies on the way here, did you?" I joke.

"Nope!" Marshall declares. "Do you want us to go back and check?"

"No!" I shout.

"Snickers wants to know if we have any dandelion greens," Marcus informs me.

"Dandelion greens?" I ask.

"It's his favorite," Marshall says.

"Oh. Uh. I don't think I have any on hand."

"He says you should go to the store and get some."

"Okay."

"Also, do we have any grapes?" Marshall continues.

"No grapes."

"He'll need grapes too," Marcus insists.

"For what?"

"His bedtime snack!" Marshall and Marcus echo while the three of them shake their heads at each other like I'm hopelessly dense.

"Can't he just share your banana?"

"He could, but he prefers grapes," Marcus says.

Chapter 4

The next morning

The following morning, business at the cafe is brisk. Many Crested Peaks residents who overindulged during the celebration last night are here demanding their favorite breakfast burrito.

Poppy is in the corner with her coloring book because Tom is out of town, and Damien brought her to work today.

The rabbits are showing Snickers around the town and begging the shopkeepers for treats. But when they return a short time later, Marshall approaches me, sniffing nervously.

"Hey, lady..."

"We're pretty busy right now," I point out. "Is this urgent?"

He turns back to Marcus. "Would you say this is urgent?"

"I guess not," Marcus shrugs.

"Okay, whatever it is, I'll deal with it after this rush."

Poppy interrupts. "Snickers says there's a dead guy next to the Thai One On food truck."

"Hilarious, you guys. Send your cousin in here to tell me you found another body. Don't you have some other shopkeeper to pester? I'm sure the new Italian restaurant down the street has fresh parsley for you."

"Snickers says since he's already dead, maybe it isn't urgent." Poppy interprets.

I turn to face them, hands on my hips. "You troublemakers really shouldn't bring Poppy into this. She's a little girl, and it's bad enough that you're trying to con me, but don't talk like that in front of her."

"But we always come to you when we find a body. If you're too busy, is there someone else we should tell?" Marshall asks. "Besides Poppy, I mean."

"Dude, we can try that guy she's always kissing," Marcus suggests.

"Oh yeah, the guy at the police station!" Marshall responds, nodding his head.

"C'mon, Snickers, we'll show you the police station," Marcus exclaims.

"But Drew can't hear you!" I point out. Good gravy, are we seriously having this conversation?

"Oh, yeah, I forgot about that."

"Let's go find some parsley. This is boring," Marcus says, sauntering out the door.

"Wait!" I yell at them. "You're joking, right?"

They shrug their tiny rabbit shoulders. "If you say so," Marcus responds.

Once again, they start to leave. "Stop!" I yell while people in the cafe stare back at me. I must look like a lunatic shouting at rabbits. Sure, everybody talks to their pets, but how many pets actually talk back?

"They sound serious, boss," Damien says, poking his head through the serving window.

"How do you know? You can't hear them!" I snap.

"I can hear your responses though."

I glance back at the rabbits who hesitate in the doorway, forcing people to walk around and stare down at them like they can't believe there are three rabbits just sitting there looking at me.

"Just check out the food truck. I'll keep things under control here," Damien urges.

"Fine. I'll see," I grumpily stuff my apron under the countertop. "But when there's no body, I'll be really irritated with the three of you!" I scold.

"Wishful thinking?" Damien mumbles.

"I heard that!" I call back as I follow the rabbits out the door.

Thankfully, it isn't a long walk. The trucks are all parked in the lot next to Snowball Park, down the street from the cafe. Which, coincidentally, has been the scene of many mysterious crimes in Crested Peaks.

The rabbits run ahead of me while I maintain a slow jog behind them. "I swear the three of you are in so much trouble," I tell them.

I just don't see how they could come across another body.

It's impossible.

It's unlikely.

It's... aw crap.

Chapter 5

The rabbits stop at what is most definitely a body. The body of Mayor Maxwell Doyle with a knife sticking out of his chest right next to the Thai One On food truck.

I stare at Mayor Doyle's lifeless body while I flash back to yesterday's fight where everyone commented that they've never seen Sam Bunmi that angry. This is very bad.

I not only bestow a blessing on his soul requesting a smooth journey to the afterlife, but I also whisper an incantation that can determine if a Super Natural or a Non Super Natural committed the murder. The spell can detect the presence of dark magic, but I get nothing, so a Non Super Natural must have murdered him.

Then I hear police sirens heading our direction and realize I'm about to be discovered standing over yet another body. Drew won't be happy. I consider running, but I'm not fast enough. The rabbits, however, are lightning-fast, and the moment they hear the sirens, they exclaim, "We're outta here!"

"Be back in time for dinner!" I call after them. Like they'd miss dinner.

I cringe as three patrol cars and an unmarked vehicle driven by Drew screech to a halt in front of me. I give Drew a half-hearted wave, and he shakes his head.

"Back away from the body!" an officer shouts, placing his hand on his gun.

"She's with me!" Drew assures him as he approaches. He obviously can't believe this is happening again either.

"New guy?" I ask, nodding my head toward the officer, who obviously thinks I had something to do with this.

"Yeah," he responds. "Can you at least tell me you found the body and not the rabbits?"

"Nope!"

"What's going on here?" the new guy asks.

"Charlotte Duffin, the owner of Marcall's Breakfast Cafe, discovered the body while on a walk this morning," Drew tells him.

As I said. Few people know about the talking rabbits. Fewer still would believe it, even if I told them.

"How do we know she didn't stab this man?" the new guy asks while a different officer, one I've come across many times, leans over and whispers in his ear. No doubt explaining to him who I am.

"Oh, I see," he responds, nodding his head.

Drew makes a face. "Did you touch anything?"

"I did not."

"Did you trip and fall on top of the victim?" he asks. I'll never live that one down.

"I did not. I took a break from work, to get some fresh air, and I found the body. That's all."

"You can go back to the cafe while we secure the area," he tells me.

I've done this so many times I know the drill. Drew will come to the restaurant later to update me on the case and get my official statement.

The other officers are already securing the area with the yellow crime scene tape while waiting for the medical examiner's office. A small crowd gathers taking pictures. I wonder how many of them were recording the fight yesterday, too.

I reluctantly wander back to Marcall's. I want to stick around to learn more, but I know Drew will just shoo me away. When I walk through the door, Damien, upon seeing my face, throws his hands in the air.

"You've *got* to be kidding me!"

"Nope." I shake my head.

"Who is it this time?" he asks.

"Why, who do you have in the pool?"

He looks guilty.

Rumor has it there's a betting pool in town predicting whose body I'll find next. I can't believe that people could be so crass, but I also can't believe how many dead people we've stumbled upon in the two years I've been back. Some of those literally. Like my former landlord whose body I tripped over behind the cafe.

"I don't know what you're talking about," Damien says, suddenly busying himself with the mole sauce he's making. When he was a child, his family moved here from Cuba, and he often infuses a variety of Caribbean, Latin, and South American cultures into his cooking.

It's part of what makes us so popular. That and the delicious low-calorie donut recipe that he and I invented using his culinary skills and my witchcraft.

"If you must know, it was Mayor Doyle, and stabbed by the Bunmi's food truck," I tell him.

His head snaps up, his eyes like saucers. "The same Mayor Doyle who fought with Mr. Bunmi yesterday?"

"The very same."

"Oh, that's bad."

Chapter 6

Several hours later, Aranya bursts through the cafe door. "Boss, I need your help!" she cries.

"Is it your dad?" I ask.

"Yes! Wait, how did you know?"

Gulp. What do I say now? My rabbits and their cousin found the mayor's body next to your family food truck? The same mayor who your dad punched out yesterday?

Is it tacky to admit that I thought of Aranya's dad first, when I saw the body? I don't think Mr. Bunmi actually stabbed anyone, but I've done this enough to know who the cops' primary suspect will be.

"I just kind of assumed..." I trail off, not sure what to say next.

Her shoulders slump. "You've heard."

"It's hard not to." I point out.

"Yeah, I guess you're right."

"But why would you need my help?" I ask.

"The police brought my dad in for questioning."

"I think he needs a lawyer more than he needs me."

"He insists innocent people don't need lawyers," she explains.

I understand that. Two years ago, when the police brought me in for questioning, I claimed I didn't need a lawyer. Although I probably should have requested one now that I've had plenty of time to think it over. Despite my innocence.

"But how can I help?" I ask.

"You can find out who really did this!" she begs.

Damien, always the cautious one, shakes his head. "The police are handling it," he tells her.

"You know I've sworn that off!" I remind her. "You know how Drew feels about me interfering in investigations."

"But it's my dad!" she insists.

"I understand that. I also know your dad would never do anything like that, but I can't keep playing investigator when I'm not. Do I need to remind you how you and I were almost killed last winter investigating a case?"

"Hey, what about me?" Damien exclaims.

"Yes, Damien too!" I point at him.

I have a bad habit of sticking my nose where it doesn't belong. Then it almost always ends with my life and my friends' lives hanging in the balance.

Aranya knows this firsthand, so she should understand why I can't get involved. Also, the Crested Peaks Police Department hates it when I meddle.

"Seriously? You'll investigate every other crime in Crested Peaks, but the one that involves my dad is the one you shy away from?"

"We all know," I insist, "that your dad is incapable of killing anyone. I'm sure the police will quickly come to the same conclusion and clear him. You won't even *need* my help."

"For my family's sake, you better be right!" she exclaims, turning on her heel, stomping out the door.

"Does that mean she isn't coming to work today?" Damien asks.

"I'm guessing no."

Chapter 7

Just as I'm about to close up the cafe, Drew shows up with a shocking request. "I think I may need your help with this one."

I know exactly what he's talking about. "Are you kidding me?"

"Aranya's father is our primary suspect."

"Oh no, I knew that would happen," I moan.

"Do not repeat what I'm about to tell you, Charlotte. I'm serious, not even Damien or Miranda."

"You're worrying me," I tell him. This *is* serious. He never calls me Charlotte. He also never bothers to warn me I shouldn't tell Damien or Miranda because he knows I will anyway.

"You *should* be worried. The knife that killed the mayor came from the Bunmi's food truck."

I gasp. "I still don't believe that he did it. In case you're forgetting, the rolling pin that killed *my* landlord came from *my* kitchen."

"I haven't forgotten, but remember how much trouble you were in for a while and how guilty you looked?"

"Ok, but why do you need my help?"

"People in this town trust you. They open up to you. You and those talking animals have resources and connections that the CPPD doesn't," Drew admits.

"Now you sound like Serenity," I tell him, pointing toward the candy store. "But I still can't believe you're telling me this. Aranya was here earlier, begging me to get involved, and I told her no. I said that you and the CPPD made me promise I'd never do that again. Now she's mad at me for refusing to help."

"It's not like we're swearing you in as one of CPPD's finest. You still need to be safe. Don't do anything dumb like driving out to an abandoned warehouse because you get an anonymous text message in the middle of the night."

"Okay, now you're exaggerating."

He holds up two fingers. "Barely. Just keep your ear to the ground and let me know if you discover anything important."

"Okay, if you insist."

My employee's mild-mannered dad gets into a slugfest with the mayor. Marshall and Marcus have a traveling cousin from Canada. On top of all that, Detective Andrew Bailey is requesting my help with solving a crime. What an upside-down holiday this turned out to be.

Chapter 8

The following morning at o'dark thirty - breakfast cafe time for those in the know - I help all three rabbits and Stumpy into my ancient Prius and drive to the cafe. I haven't heard anything new from Drew about Mr. Bunmi, but that isn't unusual. I barely see him when he's on an active case because he works such long hours.

When we arrive at the cafe, Damien is already there. He's made coffee, thank goodness, and is working on the day's menu. After the holiday's feeding frenzy, we're low on supplies, so a trip to the store is on the to-do list today. I'm wistful, as I recall that's typically something I'd ask Aranya to do, but she hasn't spoken to me since yesterday.

I don't blame her because, well, she's right. I get involved in every other case involving our friends, but then I refuse to help her father. But now that I have the green light from the CPPD that changes things.

I *should* help her if I can. I'm a witch and a cafe owner, I have resources and connections that the CPPD doesn't have. Aranya works for me, and she's a good friend. I owe it to her to take this seriously.

Damien and I enjoy the calm before the cafe opens, sipping coffee and eating our low-calorie, but delicious, donuts when his phone dings. He pulls it from his apron, staring down at it. I'm on high alert when his face pales.

"What? What is it? Don't tell me there's another body," I say half in jest, hoping to break the tension.

"The police have officially charged Aranya's father with murder." He thrusts the phone at me, and I see a picture of Mr. Bunmi in handcuffs, being led away from his home with a grief-stricken Aranya and her mother in the background. We have another mystery to solve.

Chapter 9

The arrest changes everything, and I find myself in the candy shop next door talking it over with Serenity. I do that a lot these days. She reminds me of my Gran.

She's level-headed, patient, and wise. The ideal person to bounce ideas off. I also love that she looks like someone who could play Mrs. Claus in a Christmas movie.

She's well-padded, as every candy maker should be, with her silver hair piled on top of her head. The lines on her face show a life well lived and speak of wisdom.

The store is exactly how you'd picture a candy store; only Serenity is a witch, so she carries all the traditional candies as you'd expect, but then she also has the enchanted ones. Red candies that whistle while you eat them, peppermint candies that make you giggle, and chocolates that turn your lips into rainbow colors for two days.

The store is so cheerful, and Stumpy says he thinks it smells of "sugar and spice and everything nice." Pink and red are the primary colors. The floor has alternating pink and white tiles, while the ice cream sundae counter has red stools and a patterned marble counter that's enchanted with swirling pink and red glittering streams that move.

There's even an old-fashioned jukebox in the corner that plays actual records. The whole place is so cozy and inviting, which is a relief after all the drama that has happened here in the past. Rita, the landlord, had to be extra careful about choosing the tenant this time, but she chose well.

"So that's the story," I tell Serenity as I chew on a piece of watermelon licorice, a new candy flavor in her shop. "This is really good." I hold the candy up before shoving the last of it into my mouth.

"I knew you'd like it," she smiles. "But where do you go from here?"

"I need to check out everybody and anybody who hated the mayor enough to kill him."

"You're *sure* that Mr. Bunmi didn't kill him?" she asks.

"I'm sure. If you met him before the unfortunate public fight with the mayor, you'd know, too. He's one of the most chill people I've ever known. I don't know what got into him at the festival."

"Money can make people do crazy things," she reminds me.

"Yeah, I know that, but I also know that he didn't do it."

"I'm guessing as a politician; the mayor racked up a lot of enemies."

I nod my head. "While I hate to speak ill of the dead, Mayor Doyle seemed rather, uh, *corrupt*," I whisper the last word.

"The list of suspects could be lengthy," she points out.

"I agree. You know I don't want Aranya counting on me alone to solve this. What if I fail her?"

She pats me on the hand. "You do the best you can. That's all she or anybody can expect. Believe in yourself and don't hesitate to ask your friends for help, and you'll be fine."

I hope she's right. I don't want to be the reason Aranya's father goes to prison. I mean, aside from actually killing someone, that is.

Chapter 10

The next morning

"Good morning, all!" Gladys announces with a dramatic flourish as she sweeps into the cafe. Gladys is Crested Peaks' gossip maven. She's a treasure trove of information I often turn to when solving crimes.

A tall, thin woman with curly gray hair who's always dressed impeccably in a matching hat and purse, she takes her role as a purveyor of community wide news very seriously.

"Welcome back! How did your trip go?" I ask. She spent the last month on an Alaskan cruise, and it hasn't been the same without her. When she isn't cruising, she's here every morning at precisely 6:30, ordering a vegan breakfast burrito and coffee, a caramel latte, with extra caramel of course, and oat milk.

"It was marvelous! Everyone should try it. Hey, I hear *you're* investigating the mayor's murder," she says, poking me in the shoulder. She laughs at my surprised look. I knew she was good, but she's barely back in town and already has the scoop.

"I must admit it, Gladys, I'm worried about Mr. Bunmi. He punched the mayor and threatened him in front of half the town, so everybody assumes he did it. Even Drew thinks the situation is so dire he gave me permission to check it out."

"So, find someone else who wanted the mayor dead," she suggests.

"You're confirming there were others?"

"Oh, honey, that list is long and distinguished."

"Okay, so who do you suggest?"

"I'd start with Conrad Hanson."

"I don't know who that is," I tell her.

"Hanson is a real estate developer who recently invested a ton of his own money in some high falootin project because Mayor Doyle swore he would support it and could convince the city council to vote with him."

"Let me guess. He backed out," I respond sarcastically.

"He didn't just back out. He shocked Hanson and everyone else by voting against it at the city council meeting. Then the council had to go along with him."

"I imagine Mr. Hanson was furious."

"Furious is an understatement - the mayor not only cost him money but humiliated him as well. Hanson bragged to anyone who would listen about how the mayor backed his project, and they would all be even richer than they already were. Then he blindsided him." Gladys shakes her head, recalling the moment.

"Please tell me he threatened the mayor," I beg.

"In front of the city council and everyone at the meeting, including a gaggle of reporters."

"Mr. Hanson is my first visit. I assume you know where I can find him?"

"But of course. He eats lunch every day at the Smoking Pepper Bar," she says.

"I bet you can tell me what he orders for lunch."

"Did you ever doubt me?" she asks.

"Never," I say with a grin.

"He orders the smoked salmon and a glass of bourbon. He takes all his meetings there. Anyone who wants to spend time with him shows up at noon, hoping to get an appointment."

"That settles it. Miranda and I are lunching at the Smoking Pepper today!" I exclaim.

It takes a little arm twisting and a promise to pay for lunch, but I finally convince Miranda to come with me to the Smoking Pepper at noon. Just like Gladys predicted, Conrad Hanson is holding court in the back corner of the restaurant.

We sit nearby and listen in while he wheels and deals with the people who show up, begging him to support their efforts. When there's a lull in the parade, we quickly slide into the chairs across from him.

"Good afternoon, ladies! I don't believe we've ever met! Conrad Hanson," he says, wiping his hand on a cloth napkin and extending it to us. We both shake his hand and introduce ourselves. He reminds me of every cliche used car salesman I've ever seen on tv.

He's a large man who wears a cowboy hat, a dark gray suit, and a red scarf around his neck. We didn't even have to strain to listen when he talked to the others; he's so loud.

"I'm looking into Mayor Doyle's, er, untimely passing, which I'm sure you've heard about." I jump in right away.

He snorts. "Who hasn't?" Then he empties his glass. "Barkeep!" he barks, holding it up to show he needs a refill. The barkeeper nods and sends a waitress over with a bottle to refill Mr. Hanson's glass. They're obviously used to dealing with him.

"I understand that you and the mayor weren't on speaking terms."

"Eh, it's all water under the bridge," he insists, waving his hand like it was nothing more than a mixed-up coffee order.

"What exactly happened between you two?" I press.

"I approached Max with a proposal for developing the old Johnson place. I wanted to convert it into a spa."

"What kind of spa?"

"A beauty spa. You know, one of them fancy places with massages, facials, hair styling, things you ladies are probably into."

When I see Miranda open her mouth, no doubt to correct his rather inappropriate assumption, I kick her foot under the table. No need to get into that now. We have a murder to solve.

"Hey, can I get you gals a drink?" he asks, nodding at his glass.

"Sure," Miranda says as I kick her under the table again. We're not here to socialize.

"Stop kicking me," she mutters, giving me the angry side-eye.

"You thought people in Crested Peaks would enjoy visiting a beauty spa in town?" I ask.

"Well, heck yeah. Why wouldn't they? After a day of skiing, people would love to come back and relax at the spa. I also had plans to include an elegant restaurant. My company's costly developmental studies guaranteed it would be a raging success."

"Mayor Doyle supported all of this?"

"You're a curious little thing, ain't ya?" he chuckles.

At 5 feet 10, it's rare that someone refers to me as little, although compared to Mr. Hanson, I suppose I am.

I'm concerned when I realize that the more I question him, the sweatier and more red-faced he gets. I consider asking him about it, but that would be rude, wouldn't it?

He pulls a handkerchief from his jacket pocket and dabs himself.

"Why are you asking me all these questions? Are you a reporter?"

"No, nothing like that," I assure him. "Mr. Bunmi's daughter works for me, and as a favor to her, I'm trying to learn everything I can about the people who knew the mayor best." I decided I should be upfront with him rather than invent a cover. Mostly because I didn't create a cover before coming here.

"Max, uh, Mayor Doyle assured me he supported the project 100%. He convinced me it was already a done deal, and that the city council would go along with whatever he said - like they always did."

"So, would you say you were mad enough to kill him?"

Hanson laughs. "So that's your angle, huh? You want to know if I killed Maxwell Doyle?"

He pounds on the table, increasingly ill looking. "Hey, can I get a glass of water over here?" he shouts.

The waitress hurries over with a glass of ice water.

"Pretty much." I nod my head.

"If you want the truth, I was madder than a box of frogs, but it's not worth killing over. It's just money, after all. In fact, when that old buzzard got smoked, I was in Grand Junction on a business trip. I'm always searching for the next deal, of course. So, the answer is no, I didn't kill him."

"Is there anyone who can verify your whereabouts that night?" I ask.

"You're persistent, ain't ya? Here. Call The Morrison Group offices and ask for Billy. He'll tell you I spent the weekend there."

He slides a business card toward us, and I slip it into my pocket. I'll most definitely be following up on this later.

"If you want to know who could have killed the mayor, you should talk to Simon Pointer."

"Who's that?" Miranda asks.

"It's the mayor's kid."

"You think Mayor Doyle's kid killed him?"

He laughs so hard he wheezes, and now he's sweating through his clothes. For a second, I'm reminded of that scene from Airplane where buckets of sweat pour off Robert Hayes. But this one is real. Miranda and I quickly glance at each other. I can tell she's worried.

"Are you okay?" I ask him. "Is there someone we can call for you?"

"Nah, I'm fine, but I'm not talking about Mayor Doyle's kid. I'm talking about the other guy."

"I don't follow," I tell him. I'm desperate for more information, but Hanson's face is bright red, and I'm seriously considering calling an ambulance whether or not he wants me to.

"Didn't you wonder why they called him Mayor *pro-tem*?" he asks.

"I didn't realize they called him that." I'm distracted by the fact he's clutching the table just to remain upright.

"The original mayor went to federal prison in Lakewood for tax evasion. Doyle was the pro tem. How did you not know that?"

"I don't really follow politics," I admit.

"Well, you should. It affects you as a small business owner and a citizen of Crested Peaks."

"I'm sure you're right, but for now, why don't you just fill me in on what happened and why he has reason to hate the mayor. I mean the current mayor. Er, I mean the deceased mayor. This is getting complicated. If he's in prison, how could he kill Doyle?"

"He couldn't have, but his son could."

"What does that have to do with Mayor Doyle?" This is all so confusing, and he's making me antsy. I wish he'd just get to the point.

"Mayor Doyle ratted out Pointer so he could take over."

"Oh, got it."

"That left the mayor's son and wife to clean up all the pieces. The feds took everything. They lost a pile of money and their house."

"You think that could be a reason to kill?"

"Don't you?" he laughs wheezing even harder.

"I don't care what he says. He needs help," Miranda whispers.

"I'm thinking the same thing," I whisper back.

Just as I reach for my phone to call for an ambulance, Hanson declares, "I don't feel so great." Then he presses a meaty hand to his chest and collapses.

Chapter 11

He grabs at the next table to catch himself, but instead, he pulls it down, sending everything on it flying.

Drinks, hamburgers, fries, oh my, land on the people who, until that point, were enjoying their lunch. The noise from the crashing table and breaking glass sends everyone running. One lady even screams when she sees Mr. Hanson lying on the floor, ketchup dripping from his face, and a french fry stuck to his balding head.

Miranda calls 911, which we should have done at least 10 minutes ago.

"Excuse me! I'm a nurse!" a man shouts, elbowing his way through the crowd of onlookers. "Make way, please! This man needs medical attention!" He begs, "Please! Give him some room! He needs room!"

I still regret my hesitation during the fight on Independence Day, and I refuse to make the same mistake twice. I quickly use witchcraft to erect an invisible barrier around Conrad Hanson and the nurse. People are pushed back without realizing why.

Miranda smiles at me and nods her head. I can tell she's impressed. She should be. She taught me that spell.

The nurse checks for a pulse and immediately begins CPR. Is it horrible that I immediately realize if he killed the mayor, and now he dies too, we may never know the truth?

What if my questions made him so nervous, they killed him? I wonder if Drew has ever experienced this with a suspect.

The ambulance arrives within minutes, and the EMTs make their way through the restaurant crowd. I lift the enchanted barrier so they can get through.

They use a defibrillator on him, and when his heart starts again, I breathe a sigh of relief. He isn't out of the woods yet, but at least his heart is beating. They load him onto the stretcher and hurry out the door.

With Hanson on his way to the hospital, customers return to their tables and the wait staff cleans up the mess left behind. Meanwhile the manager assures the couple, still covered in their own lunch, that they can come back any time for a meal and drinks on the house.

"Are you ladies, okay?" he asks as I pluck a lemon wedge from Miranda's blouse collar.

"A little rattled, but we're fine," Miranda assures him, pulling a straw wrapper out of my hair.

"The same goes for you, too. Come back anytime for a free lunch, okay?" he tells us.

Miranda and I head out into the hot July afternoon sun, squinting after being in the darkened bar. I know people don't believe me when I tell them that trouble just seems to find me, but I swear the proof is there. What a wild lunch that turned out to be.

"What do you think?" Miranda asks as we stroll down the sidewalk back to Marcall's. My pulse is still racing from all the excitement.

"I think that seriously freaked me out."

"Not *that* you dolt," she says, smacking me on the arm. "I mean about Hanson as a suspect. Do you think he could have done it?"

"He lost a lot of money because of Mayor Doyle."

"Plus, the humiliation," she reminds me. "That's motive."

"We need to check out his alibi, though," I insist.

"You still have the card he gave you? You didn't lose it in all the excitement, did you?"

"Got it right here!" I wave it in front of her.

Damien rushes me the moment I walk in the door to Marcall's. "Is it true?" he asks breathlessly.

"Is what true?"

"You found another body?"

I glare at the rabbits in the corner, who are snickering uncontrollably.

"No, I didn't find another body!" I insist.

"So, you killed Conrad Hanson?" he whispers, shock clouding his face.

"I didn't kill anybody! Where are you getting this?"

"It's all over town. You and Miranda were questioning Conrad Hanson at the Smoking Pepper about the mayor's murder, and then you killed him. Or you found his body in the alley. There are two different stories making the rounds."

"We started the one about the body in the alley," Marcus laughs.

"We were asking him about his relationship to Mayor Doyle, and he got all red and sweaty and keeled over. The ambulance came and took him away. But they got his heart started again before they left." I quickly add. "I can't believe people are already talking about this! We barely left there!"

"You know how the gossip train works in this town." Damien reminds me.

"It doesn't help that you're telling stories about me either!" I waggle my finger at the rabbits, who run off to the back room, laughing the entire way. What, you've never heard a rabbit laugh?

Chapter 12

"So, what *really* happened? Did you learn anything?" Damien asks.

Just as I'm about to launch into my story, Drew throws open the door to the café, relieved to see me standing there in one piece.

"I assumed *most* of the rumors were false, but I wanted to double-check for myself."

"Which rumors did *you* hear?" I ask.

"Uhhhh, let's see, as of an hour ago, you used a special potion to poison Conrad Hanson's bourbon, and then you used magic to burn down the Smoking Pepper..."

"They're getting wilder," Damien points out. "I heard she found another body in the alley."

"I heard that one too, but since the CPPD didn't get a call on that, I dismissed it."

"But you believed the one where I burned down the Smoking Pepper?" I ask.

"I didn't believe that one either," Drew says, hugging me. Not much of an apology if you ask me.

"I just hope Conrad is okay," I tell them.

He nods his head. "I heard from my source at the hospital. He had a heart attack and needs a triple bypass, but assuming he survives the surgery, he should be fine. Although he should also cut back on the bourbon lunches."

"So, it really wasn't my fault," I breathe a sigh of relief. "Unless I'm the one who brought on the heart attack because I was getting too close to exposing him as the murderer."

"Even if he is the murderer, his heart attack wouldn't be your fault," Drew points out.

"Tell that to the people who are saying she killed him!" Damien says. I glare at him. "I didn't say *I* said that, just *the people*." He holds his hands up in surrender.

"Hey, how long has it been since we all had dinner together?" I ask.

"I think Thanksgiving?" Damien responds.

"That long? That's horrible! Why don't you all come over tonight so we can brainstorm the case?"

"I have to double-check with Tom, but I don't think we have plans otherwise," Damien says.

"I'm game!" Drew responds.

"Great! I'll invite Miranda and Miles too."

Aside from all the drama, did you learn anything important from Mr. Hanson? Do you think he killed Mayor Doyle?" Damien asks.

"He claims that all the money the mayor cost him isn't a big deal, and he's over it."

"But you don't believe him?" Drew asks.

"Here's the thing. Conrad Hanson spent a *lot* of money determining whether a luxury spa in Crested Peaks would be worth it. All based on Mayor Doyle telling him it was a great idea, that he was totally on board, and the city council would support him no matter what. In addition to the money, he's already out, he counted on the future income, which disappeared once the mayor unexpectedly backed out."

"He must have been livid when the mayor blindsided him at the meeting," Drew says.

"Exactly," I respond.

"I saw it on the news," Damien adds. "He went berserk. Let me see if I can find it." He pulls out his phone and does a quick search. "Oh yeah, here it is. This thing went viral within hours."

Damien shows me the video. The moment the mayor voted no, Hanson leaped from his seat, screaming, "What in the sam hill?"

Then, as each council person voted no, his rage intensified. When he realized they had voted down the proposal 6-0, he shouted expletives and threw chairs.

He even rushed the dais where the council sits, grabbed the papers sitting in front of them, and flung them. One of them had a coffee cup, that he picked up and smashed on the ground.

Definitely not the guy who spent our meeting trying to convince me that it wasn't a big deal. It took three security guards to capture him and drag him from the room.

The last thing he shouted before they pulled him out the door was, "I'll kill you! I swear I'll kill you, Doyle. I'll stab you in the heart just like you did to me!"

I stare at Damien in horror.

"He doesn't look like someone who thinks it isn't a big deal," Damien says.

"Can I point out here that Hanson is way angrier in this video than Mr. Bunmi was when they were fighting," I say. "Since the spa proposal didn't pass, what are they doing with the property? Anything?"

"They're turning it into mini-golf." Drew says.

"You're joking."

"Nope. The following month, they voted on a mini-golf course."

"Which Hanson doesn't own, correct?"

"Nope. The mayor's brother-in-law owns that."

"That guy was a piece of work, wasn't he?"

"What else did he tell you?" Damien asks. "Or was that when you killed him?"

"Ha ha. You're a comedian. But now that you mention it, he thinks the former mayor's son, or possibly even his wife, could have done it."

"Nice of him to point the finger at someone else."

"That's what I thought, but it's worth checking out. Mayor Doyle truly betrayed Conrad Hanson but I'd say what he did to Mayor Pointer, and his family was far worse. I just need to figure out where I can find this Pointer guy. Perhaps his mother too."

"I think he's an insurance salesman. Just do an internet search for him," Damien suggests.

I do, and sure enough, his office is two blocks away. Let's hope I don't give this guy a heart attack, too.

Chapter 13

I tap lightly on Simon Pointer's office door. "Excuse me, Mr. Pointer?"

"Yes," he sighs, his voice heavy with annoyance. This is going great so far.

"I'm Charlotte Duffin, and I own Marcall's Breakfast Cafe."

"And?"

"I wanted to talk to you about Mayor Doyle for a moment."

"Why, are you a friend of his? You aren't welcome here, and I don't want to hear about it."

"No, I never even met the mayor. But Mr. Bunmi's daughter works for me, and as you can imagine, the family is in chaos right now. I'm trying to find out as much as possible about what might have happened that night."

"If you ask me, I'd say Bunmi deserves a medal."

"Why's that?"

"For killing that no good cheating snake."

"I take it you and the mayor weren't friendly?"

"Honey, that's the understatement of the year. I hated that guy. I danced a happy little dance when I heard he died."

"That's kind of harsh, don't you think?"

"Nope! Not after what he did to my family. Mayor Doyle," when he says the word "Mayor," he sneers, "is the reason my father is in prison right now."

"But I thought your dad went prison for tax evasion." I point out.

"Yes, my old man cheated on his taxes."

"I think if he's in a federal penitentiary, he did more than simply cheat on his taxes. With all due respect," I add on quickly.

Pointer nods and rolls his eyes. "Fair enough. My old man played fast and loose with the feds and lost. How's that? But not until Doyle ratted him out to the authorities so *he* could become mayor. My poor mother is so distraught we had her committed."

Hanson didn't mention that part. "I'm so sorry. How is she doing now?"

"She catatonic. She's at the Baker facility, and all she does is stare into space. Even when I visit, she doesn't seem to know me."

There goes my plan to question his mom.

"Is it permanent?" I ask.

"They don't know. We have the best doctors money can buy, and even they can't tell us anything."

"Forgive me if this is indelicate, but it's my understanding that your family lost everything. The federal government confiscated it all. How can you afford these high-priced doctors?"

"My mom's family is paying for it," he answers with a snide tone.

"Ah, I see."

"We lost our money, our house, and my mom lost her marbles, I guess you could say."

"I don't suppose I could try talking to your mom? It wouldn't take long." I mention as delicately as I can.

"Why? What good would that do?"

"I'm not sure, but I think it might be important to get her perspective."

"I'd tell you to go ahead and try, but the hospital isn't allowing her to have any visitors right now other than me."

"Oh. I see."

"You think I killed Doyle? I didn't." He snaps at me.

"But you hated him enough to kill him if you had the chance?" I ask.

He shifts nervously in his seat. He may talk a good game about how much he hated the mayor, but it's entirely different to confess to killing him.

"I'll be honest with you, Ms., uh, what did you say your name is?"

"Charlotte Duffin."

"I'll be honest with you, Ms. Duffin. I certainly thought about killing him. Especially after my mom got sick. But, again, no, I didn't kill him," he insists, his agitation growing.

"You know I have to ask where you were the night Mayor Doyle was murdered."

"I went camping in Washington Gulch."

"By yourself?"

"Yep. All alone."

His clipped tone tells me I'm wearing out my welcome, but I'm not quite finished. Who camps alone? Granted, I won't even go camping with other people, but I certainly wouldn't camp alone. What if a bear showed up? Or a snake? Or even a spider? *Blech*. No thanks.

"Sure! I do it all the time. It helps me clear my head. Spend a couple of nights in the woods with no cell phone or tv. Just fresh air and a campfire. It's great. You should try it sometime."

"Yeah, I'll have to consider that, but isn't there anyone who saw you? A park ranger or another camper? Perhaps you stopped to get gas or supplies on your way there? A receipt would help."

I'm grasping at straws here but why won't he give me more information? Something that could prove his innocence?

"Nope," he insists, shaking his head. "I didn't interact with anyone else the entire time."

"You said you were in the Washington Gulch campground?"

"That's correct."

Just as I'm about to give up I watch the blood drain from his face. I swear if this guy has a heart attack, too, I quit.

"What are you doing here?" he growls.

"Now, is that any way to talk to your friends, Simon?" a man behind me asks.

I spin around in my chair, my hand against my chest; I'm so startled. I stare up at two scruffy men who must have snuck in behind me. They ooze equal parts, smarmy and creepy. Yuck.

"Who's this pretty little lady?" the other one asks, leering down at me. If this guy so much as thinks about putting a finger on me, I'll hex him. Sure, I'm not so great with the hexing, but I could set his hair on fire. That would be fun. People would really have something to talk about then.

"None of your business. What do you want?" Pointer asks.

"We don't appreciate your attitude, Simon," the guy with greasy hair says.

"Are we done here?" Simon asks me.

"Yes, well, thanks for answering my questions, and if you think of anything, could you please let me know? I hope your mom gets better soon."

"Yeah, thanks," he says with the most insincere thanks I've ever heard.

I wish I could ask him more, but I don't want to stick around with these two in the office. They strike me as loan shark types. Maybe Simon owes them money.

Or he has an illegal deal with them. Perhaps Simon is a chip off the old block, and they're involved with some illegitimate business dealings. Whatever it is, I'm out of here. I don't want to be in the same room with them.

Chapter 14

"Drew, can you get the…never mind, I got it," I tell him as I levitate a bottle of wine and a charcuterie tray out the back door to the patio table.

"Whoa!" he exclaims, dodging to avoid getting beaned in the head.

"Oh yeah, duck!" I laugh.

"Way to make a guy feel useless," he tells me.

"Sorry about that. I just automatically think of witchcraft now. At least for the simple tasks, it seems like. Now, if I could do it without hesitating on the difficult stuff."

"I'm a cop, and I know it takes practice. I would say it's kind of like a muscle memory thing. If you're under duress often enough, it becomes second nature."

"Good to know," I tell him. "That's actually very helpful."

"Don't take that as permission to purposely put yourself in harm's way just to practice, though!"

"Also duly noted." I nod my head.

When the doorbell rings, I tell him I do need his help with the door.

"Finally! Something I can assist with!"

I hear Damien and Tom and Poppy at the front door. "Stumpy, where are you?" is the first thing Poppy says when she walks in. Meanwhile, I watch Stumpy tiptoe down the hallway to hide. You wouldn't think that a two-footed cat could tiptoe, would you?

Poppy likes to dress the boys in costumes and play tea party with them. Marcus and Marshall tell me they tolerate her because she's a little girl, but they're relieved when she goes home. They think the princess crowns and fairy wings are undignified.

Bubbles, Tom and Damien's rescued bull terrier mix, marches over to the couch, flops down, and immediately falls asleep. I remind the boys that they're lucky. Bubbles must play dress-up all the time at home. Although she doesn't seem to mind. Today she's wearing butterfly wings decorated with glitter.

I inherited Gran's, Queen Anne house, which I have always loved. It has a massive wrap-around porch surrounded by incredible mountain views where I like to hang out and drink coffee on Sunday mornings when the cafe is closed.

My Gran turned the backyard into an oasis with a waterfall and a koi pond that maintains the perfect temperature year-round, thanks to a bit of witchcraft. The same goes for all the landscaping with colorful wildflowers blooming year-round.

I added my own touch with a special spell that keeps the yard free of mosquitos and flies. Oh, and wasps. Nasty little buggers, those guys are. Basically, it's perpetual summer in my backyard. Perfect for nights like this when I'm entertaining.

"Hey, I brought a Pinot Noir," Damien tells me.

"Fabulous! You can take it out to the patio."

"Where did Tom go?" I ask.

"He and Drew are already deep in discussion about football," Damien says, rolling his eyes.

"Isn't that like two months away?" I ask.

"Pre-season starts in a month!" Drew shouts.

"I stand corrected," I tell Damien.

"All right, what did you do to the patio?" Damien wonders when he comes back into the kitchen.

"Huh?"

"The temperature is perfect, and there isn't a fly or mosquito to be found."

"Ohhh, that!" I respond with a wave of my hand. "Just a little spell I conjured. The temperature is a perfect 72 degrees, and the bugs are all off pestering someone else."

Shortly after that Miles and Miranda show up with even more wine. These people know me.

"Attention, everyone! The parade is starting!" Poppy announces.

We all pause as she runs back down the hallway to the guest bedroom.

She returns, waving a small purple flag and blowing into a plastic kazoo with Marshall, Marcus, Snickers, and Stumpy trailing behind, looking none too pleased. Bubbles watches from the couch, and even though I can't talk to her, I'd swear she's relieved she doesn't have to be part of the procession.

The animals are wearing the make-shift costumes that Poppy dug out of the trunk I keep just for her. If that trunk disappears unexpectedly one of these days, I'll bet on the rabbits.

"Snickers may be second-guessing this vacation," I whisper to Damien, who laughs.

Poppy and the animals parade down the hallway, circle the living room and the kitchen, and then head back up the hallway, and we all applaud.

"We better get a lot of parsley for this!" Marshall insists.

"And with that, I think dinner is ready!" I announce.

"Poppy, take off the animals' costumes and thank them for being a part of your parade!" Tom calls back to her.

"Okay!" she says.

"Are you sure they don't mind?" Damien asks me.

"Oh, they're fine. She isn't hurting them. She's very gentle with them, and remember they can talk to her, and if it's too much, they'll tell her!"

"Fair enough," Damien says.

Dinner is simple. I'm investigating a murder, after all. Penne Alla Vodka, buttery rolls, and a tossed salad are all made with fresh ingredients from the garden. Except for the rolls. Those came from the grocery store. Did I mention I'm investigating a murder?

"Hey Charlotte, we're having an early morning meeting at the library tomorrow. Is it okay if we have it and breakfast at the cafe?" Miles asks.

Miles is Miranda's boyfriend, who she started dating shortly after I returned to Crested Peaks. He's the town librarian and has also been helpful when investigating mysteries. It's always good to have friends who know things.

"Of course! We'd love to have you. How many people?"

"I think there will be six of us."

"That's no problem."

"Any news on Hanson's triple bypass surgery?" I ask Drew because I know he has a contact at the hospital who gives him information that he probably isn't supposed to have, but who am I to complain?

"Surgery went well, and they said he's already awake and complaining that they won't let him order cocktails in the hospital."

"Now that he's on the mend, people should stop talking about you, right?" Miles says.

Miranda elbows him, giving him a salty stare.

"What? What are you talking about?" I ask.

"I told you not to say anything yet!" Miranda says, waving her hand at him.

"He wasn't supposed to say anything about what?" I ask again.

Miranda sighs. "I overheard some people in the coffee shop gossiping about how you not only have a knack for finding dead bodies, but now you're actually killing them."

"What? That's preposterous!"

"That's what I told them. Right before I threw them out." She boasts.

"You threw out customers for me?"

"Eh, they're idiots!" Miranda waves her hand dismissively.

"They're calling you the grim reaper," Marcus tells me as he begs Drew for parsley and basil.

"Did you just make that up?"

"Nope, Stumpy said he overheard it while chasing mice in the alley."

"Great! I knew this would happen!" I throw my hands in the air. They not only have a betting pool on the next body I'll find, but now they're accusing me of causing it.

"Those people aren't important," Miranda insists. "Just stick to your investigation and don't worry about what they think. Did you follow up with the contact that Hanson gave us? The one who could corroborate his alibi."

"I had Drew call him," I explain. "I felt like an official call from the CPPD might convince the guy to be more forthcoming."

"And?"

I nod my head at Drew, who replies, "He says Conrad was *not* there this weekend like he claimed. He was supposed to be there but canceled at the last minute!"

"You're kidding!" Damien exclaims.

"Nope."

"So, you've already caught him in a lie!"

"We sure have," I respond rather smugly.

"We have to go back and talk to him again. Confront him!" Miranda exclaims.

"Hey, could you avoid killing him this time?" Damien asks while Drew chokes on his beer, trying not to laugh.

"Isn't that getting old?" I ask him.

"No, ma'am, that will never get old."

"You have a point, though. I'm a little nervous now. What if I pressed him too hard before? Plus, I don't want to give people in Crested Peaks any more reason to call me the grim reaper."

Drew interrupts. "My contact told me they warned Hanson for months that he needed to get healthy, or he'd have a heart attack. Your questions didn't *cause* the heart attack."

"More like the final straw, right?" Tom says.

"Yes, exactly," Drew nods his head. "If it hadn't been your questioning, it could have been someone cutting in line at the grocery store or a lost package at the post office."

"I'm not sure that makes me feel much better. But now that I know he lied to us about his alibi, it could mean he's the killer. What if the stress of knowing he killed the mayor, and was about to get caught, finally gave him a heart attack!" I exclaim.

"That still wouldn't be our fault," Miranda points out. "How did your talk go with Simon Pointer?"

"Conrad Hanson may be obnoxious, but there's something downright creepy about Pointer."

"How so?" Drew asks.

"He doesn't even try to cover how much he hated Mayor Doyle."

"Unlike Hanson, who claimed it wasn't a big deal." Miranda reminds us.

"Right. Pointer said that Mr. Bunmi should get a medal for killing Doyle and that he danced when he heard the news."

"Whoa," Tom whispers. "He admitted that?"

"Yes, he did. Even said he low-key wished he'd done it himself."

"So, is he saying that to make it look like a guilty person would never talk like that?" Damien asks. "Was he trying to make you think he could never say that if he killed him when he really did kill him, hoping to throw you off his trail?"

"I don't know. But he's very suspicious acting if you ask me."

"Even though you know Hanson is lying?"

"I think so, yes."

"When you consider what Mayor Doyle did to Pointer's family, I'd say it's far worse than what he did to Conrad. Sure, he lost money on the deal, but Simon and his mom lost their money and their home, and Mrs. Pointer had a nervous breakdown and is still hospitalized!"

"I heard rumors about that but wasn't sure if they were true!" Miles exclaims.

"He says she's catatonic and doesn't even recognize him when he visits her, which is a shame because I'd really like to talk to her, too. I want to know if she knew her husband was deceiving the feds, in which case she'd be extra mad at Doyle. Or was she unaware of her husband's shady dealings because then she'd be madder at him, right?"

"You can't even *try* talking to her?" Miranda asks.

"Simon said he's the only visitor who's allowed. Besides even if they let me see her, I'm worried I'll say the wrong thing, and who knows what could happen. I already caused a heart attack. I don't want to send some poor woman over the edge. Who knows what she could do?"

"Did you ask his whereabouts when Mayor Doyle was killed?" Miranda asks.

"He says he went camping to clear his head." I explain nonchalantly.

"He went camping all alone?" Drew asks.

"That's what he told me." I shrug. "In Washington Gulch."

"Are you sure he said Washington Gulch?"

"Yes. I'm certain. I asked twice to confirm. Why?"

"That area has been closed for weeks because of mudslides from the spring runoff." Drew responds.

"Could he have hiked in?" I ask.

"No, there's nowhere accessible on foot. You have to drive in to reach it. And as I said, it's closed anyway."

"So that's the second guy who lied to us!" I exclaim.

"Is there anything else that made you suspicious of Simon?" Miles asks.

"That wasn't already enough?" Miranda laughs.

"There is something else." I add.

"Ha!" Miles shouts while Miranda shakes her head.

"Just as I decide our conversation is going nowhere, these two super sketchy guys show up, and Simon clearly wasn't happy about it. They made the hair on the back of my neck stand up. Gave me the big time heebie-jeebies."

Drew's brow knits with concern. "What did they say? Can you describe them? I told you to be careful about this!"

"She's never careful enough if you ask me," Damien *tsks* while Drew nods at him. "Neither of them are," he adds, waving his finger between Miranda and me.

"They barely said anything except I could tell they were up to no good. I think they were loan sharks, or he's like his dad, and he's involved in something shady."

"So, he knew them?" Drew asks.

"He absolutely knew them. They told him it was no way to treat a friend. Then they asked about me, but I got out of there without answering."

"Char, I don't want you endangering yourself over this. Don't make me regret asking for your help." Drew warns.

"I'm fine. I was all ready to set their hair on fire, if necessary," I reassure him. Not that I really would, but I don't want him to worry.

"Does anyone know how Aranya and her mom are doing?" Tom interjects. "I know that none of you think Mr. Bunmi could have done this, but how did his knife end up in Doyle's chest anyway? Someone had to have taken the knife from the food truck, right? How did someone who wasn't a Bunmi get their hands on it?"

Tom's question hangs over all of us like a dark cloud.

"Mrs. Bunmi swears her husband was home all night. And right after we found the body, I tried the door to the food truck, and it was locked. I also asked Mr. Bunmi to check out the truck, and he swears nothing was out of place. So, the short answer is, we don't know how the killer got the knife, but we know it belongs in the food truck otherwise.

"Aranya is spending most of her time with her mother, so I haven't had a chance to talk to her about how the investigation is going. She still isn't exactly thrilled with me that I hesitated to investigate this in the first place," I add with a wistful tone.

"Okay, everyone!" Poppy announces. "Time for another parade!" She has somehow convinced all three rabbits, Stumpy, and Bubbles, to ride in the large wagon we often take to events for the cafe.

Stumpy glares at Bubbles, who takes up at least half of the wagon, while the four of them squeeze into the other half. Bubbles smooshed face sports a huge grin while her tongue hangs out, panting with excitement.

"I guess we're all going for a walk!" I exclaim. We all get up and head out the door with Poppy. Dessert and the dishes can wait. Miranda and I will just use witchcraft on the dishes, anyway. We all parade down the block with Poppy and the animals leading the way.

I don't want to admit it out loud, but after Conrad's heart attack, I'm reluctant to continue questioning any suspects. It's bad enough I put him in the hospital.

Imagine if he had died? I don't know that I could forgive myself. Even if his doctors were already telling him to get healthy.

Why can't I just stick with being a successful cafe owner? Is that too much to ask?

Chapter 15

"Hey, Charlotte!"

"Miles! Nice to see you again so soon."

"We're here for our meeting, the one I told you about last night."

"Come on in, everybody! Can I get anything started for you?" I step back overwhelmed when they all call out orders at once.

"All right, guys! Don't freak out, Charlotte. One at a time." Miles holds up his hands, calling for order.

They line up to place their orders, then push several tables together in the corner.

Miles and another woman I've never met wait by the cash register to collect everyone's breakfast.

"Hi!" I say to her.

"Oh, where are my manners? Charlotte, this is Nan Leblanc, and she's the school librarian at Crested Peaks Elementary."

"Hi! Good to meet you!"

"Hey, aren't you the one who found the mayor's body?" she asks.

That came out of left field. Maybe she had the mayor in the betting pool. My heart rate spikes while I wait for her to ask if I tried to kill Conrad Hanson too.

"Yes, I am."

Miles tries to explain, sensing my discomfort over being questioned by a total stranger. "Nan had her own problems with Doyle."

"You don't say?" How long is this list? Did *anyone* like this guy? "What did he do to you?"

"He promised me funding for a mobile children's library."

"That would be so cool! Let me guess. He didn't come through?"

"Nope," Nan shakes her head. "Get this. The money he swore was earmarked for the mobile library went to commissioning a statue of himself. When I confronted him, he said oh well, those were the breaks.

"He didn't tell me he'd *consider* funding the library. He *promised* me it would happen. Swore it was a done deal. I guaranteed the parents and their kids that it would be available this summer. My school principal sent out a big announcement and everything. I'm still mad about it."

I nod my head in solidarity. "If it makes you feel any better, the more I investigate this case, the longer the list gets. Mayor Doyle had a lot of enemies."

Her eyes grow wide. "You're seriously investigating his murder? I thought the guy with the food truck did it."

I blush. I didn't mean to make myself appear more involved than I am. Or than I'm supposed to be anyway.

"Don't get me wrong. I'm not the police or anything. It's just that Mr. Bunmi is Aranya's dad, and she works for me."

"Ohhhhh, I see."

Before we can chat more about her issues with Mayor Doyle, Damien has already passed out everyone's breakfast, and the group gathers to begin their meeting.

I assumed we'd talk more later, but by the time I realize their meeting is done, Miles was the only one left.

"So, Miles, how serious was this argument between Nan and Mayor Doyle?"

"She was livid!" he tells me. "I've known her a long time and never seen her so angry."

"Really!" I exclaim eagerly.

He narrows his eyes at me. "Wait a minute. You don't think she's a suspect, do you? I'm telling you it's impossible. She's incapable of killing someone. She's the type of person who goes out of her way to take spiders outside rather than stepping on them."

He shakes his head when I look at him with skepticism.

"Yes, I know, she was hugely embarrassed over the entire thing. Her school principal was mad that she had to backtrack to all the parents about why the mobile library wasn't happening, but that's no reason to kill someone!" He continues to insist.

"I suppose you're right. Although what if she just meant to scare the mayor and things got out of hand, and she *accidentally* killed him?" I ask, hoping he'll think this is a legitimate theory.

"I'm telling you, Charlotte. It would never happen."

"I don't suppose you know her whereabouts last weekend?"

Miles shrugs. "I didn't see her before the holiday, so I don't know. The school library is open all summer, though, because the mobile library fell through. If you feel that strongly about it, you could go to the library and ask her. I guarantee it wasn't her, though. Imagine a school librarian murdering someone! It just couldn't happen."

Driving home that afternoon, my mind churns over the conversations I had with Simon and Conrad. I know that they both lied about their whereabouts when the mayor was murdered, but why? They couldn't have both done it, right? Or could they? What if they're working together?

I should confront Conrad and Simon about their lies. Although I hope Conrad is healthy enough to talk to me this time. Pus I really want to know who those creeps in Simon's office were.

In addition to those two, I now consider Nan a suspect, too. I don't care what Miles thinks. In fact, I'm going to pay her a visit at the elementary school library.

Hopefully, it's less chaotic than the cafe, and we can talk in more detail. I swear at times, it seems like I'm herding rabbits. I don't know how Drew does it.

By the time I arrive home, I'm so convinced that either Conrad or Simon, or both, are guilty that I call Drew.

"Hey, beautiful!" he says when he answers the phone.

I'm so focused ongoing after these guys that I ignore the compliment and get right to the point. "I've been thinking a lot about everything we discussed last night, and I'm sure that Conrad and Simon are hiding something important. Don't you think I should talk to them again?"

"If you're that convinced something suspicious is going on with them, I think it's best if I talk to them this time," Drew says.

"If you insist," I tell him. I'm still nervous about all of this. Best to let the professionals handle it. Also, best not to tell Drew I just thought that because he's always lecturing me on it, anyway.

I've lost count of the number of times he has scolded me about staying out of police business. "Leave this to the professionals, Char," he nags me. So there. I'm leaving it to the professionals.

I'm convinced that once the CPPD questions these two, one of them will crack, and we'll have our actual killer. Sam Bunmi can finally go free, and I can return to doing nothing but serving customers at Marcall's.

Chapter 16

While I'm catching up on some neglected laundry, I get a text from Drew.

We're bringing in Simon Pointer for questioning now. The criminal database flagged him for a recent arrest, which makes him even more suspicious.

"Yes!" I call out to no one in particular. Why was he arrested? I bet it had something to do with the skeevy guys in his office. What does he mean by recently? Yesterday? Last week? Last month? I need more detail!

I text back. **What about Conrad?**

I'm waiting to get permission from the hospital to talk to him. But I have a hunch about Simon, so I'll start with him.

A hunch?

I'll tell you more about it later.

If anybody can break him, it will be Drew. I knew that guy was no good, and now they can arrest for murder before dinner time. I'm more optimistic than I have been in a while.

I'm finishing the last of my laundry when someone pounds on my front door. What on earth? Who could be so frantic? I look through the peephole. It's Aranya!

"What up? What's wrong?" I ask, opening the door quickly.

"The bank called in the loan on my parents' food truck! We have 48 hours to pay the entire thing back, or they take the truck."

"What? Can they do that?"

"They insist it was in the fine print. If something happens that makes the bank think my parents can't afford the loan payments, they can demand my parents pay back the entire loan in two days."

"That's crazy!"

"I know. They've never been late on a payment. They always pay early. They have perfect credit," she wails loudly.

"But the bank called in the loan because of your dad's arrest." It dawns on me.

"Yes! They claim they don't think my parents can continue to make the payments with my dad in jail for murdering the mayor."

"So, if we could find the real killer, maybe the bank would change their minds because your parents could return to business as usual," I offer hopefully.

"I hope so!"

"I have some good news on that front."

"You found the real killer already?"

"I think so."

"Are you serious? Why didn't you tell me?" she exclaims growing more excited by the moment.

"The police are still sewing everything up, but do you know Simon Pointer?"

"The name sounds familiar. Wait, wasn't his dad the mayor but went to jail for tax evasion or something like that?"

"Yes!"

"If anybody had a reason to kill the mayor, it would be him, right?" Aranya asks, so hopefully that I start to feel guilty. But I'm sure it's him so I won't worry.

"I'm sure of it!" I insist.

"How did you find out? What do you know?"

"Conrad Hanson--"

"--the guy you almost killed..."

"I didn't almost kill him! Anyway, Hanson suggested I talk to Pointer. When I did, he admitted he wanted him dead. Mayor Doyle ruined his family, and he danced when he heard he was dead."

"He seriously told you that!" she exclaims in shock.

"Yes! When I asked him where he was the night Doyle was killed, he claimed he went camping alone in the Washington Gulch campgrounds and that no one saw him."

"That's suspicious," she says, her eyes narrowing.

"That's what I thought too, and it gets better. When I mentioned it to Drew, he told me Washington Gulch has been closed for weeks because of the mudslides from the spring runoff.

"He has no reason to lie about his location that night unless he's covering for something." Aranya's face lights up so much I can't help but continue. "Drew also told me there's a recent arrest on his record."

"For what?" she gasps.

"I don't know, but it can't be good, right? I'm pretty sure Simon killed Mayor Doyle, and Drew will arrest him soon."

Aranya hugs me. "Oh, Charlotte, you're so good at this. My family is forever grateful. I'm going to tell my mom right now!"

When she rushes out the door, I desperately hope I'm right. I hope I can do this because I don't want to disappoint them. I'm sure Pointer had something to do with killing the mayor.

Chapter 17

Several hours later my phone rings and I see it's Drew. My heart skips a beat.

"Please tell me you're calling to say you arrested Simon," I whisper, and cross my fingers before accepting the call.

"Hi, hot stuff!" I croon into the phone.

"Bad news," he says.

Uh, oh. "What do you mean bad news? You arrested Simon, right?"

"Simon was in jail in Blackhawk the night Doyle was killed. He can't have done it."

I'm stunned into silence, and after a lengthy pause Drew asks, "Are you still there?"

"In jail? In Blackhawk? Are you serious? Why jail? Why didn't this come up before?" I'm almost shrieking into the phone. I'm so upset.

"Holiday weekend, so the system delayed the reports. Then it got lost because they sent it to the wrong county. I just now found out. I'm so sorry. When I saw the system flagged an arrest, I didn't realize it was on July 4th."

"Why did he get arrested?"

"Card counting."

"Card counting? You can get arrested for that?"

"Well, it wasn't the literal card counting, but when the security team discovered it and asked him to leave, he grabbed a knife from the buffet and threatened to stab one of them."

"Ah ha! I knew it! He stabbed Doyle." I continue to insist.

"See, I knew that's how you'd react. But it's a coincidence. I already told you he'd been arrested," Drew says, his impatience showing.

"Oh, yeah, good point. But what if he snuck out?" I know - I'm getting desperate here.

"You're saying that he not only escaped jail, but he also drove four hours, stabbed the mayor, then drove back and snuck into the jail before anyone realized it?"

"You said it yourself - they make mistakes, and it was a holiday weekend - it could happen."

"It's so improbable that I'm unwilling to even consider it. I'm sorry, Char, but Simon Pointer isn't your guy." Drew insists.

"What am I going to tell Aranya?" I wail.

"What do you mean? What did you tell her already?"

"I told her you were on the verge of arresting Simon for the murder," I whisper.

I can just feel him pinching the bridge of his nose. "Why did you do that?" he sighs.

"She was so distraught! I wanted to make her feel better."

"You shouldn't have done that," he snaps.

"Well, I get that now!" I snap back at him.

"Okay, I have to get back to work, and you have to make things right with Aranya. I'll talk to you later."

Then the line is dead. I'm such a jerk. I shouldn't have told Aranya an arrest was imminent, and I shouldn't have just snapped at Drew like that. He was only trying to keep me updated, which considering I'm not law enforcement, he didn't really have to do.

Now Aranya's parents have only two days to pay back their truck loan. This is a disaster.

Chapter 18

Aranya was understandably upset when I told her that Simon Pointer was not our guy, and the police released him after questioning. I should have never led her on about an imminent arrest.

She was so hopeful, and I didn't want to take that away at the time. So I took it away later instead. I wanted to bring her dad back and restore their family business. Instead, I made things worse by being wishy-washy. Drew is right when he reminds me, I'm not a cop.

To make matters even worse, I caught snippets here and there this morning in the cafe and on the sidewalk along Main Street, where I'm sure people are staring at me because they think I tried to kill Conrad Hanson.

I catch pieces of whispered conversation. "Don't you think it's weird that she finds all the bodies?" "There have been so many since she moved back." "I heard she tried to kill some guy, but it didn't work." "What's up with those weird rabbits of hers?"

Sometimes I hate small-town life.

The thought of agitating Conrad Hanson again makes me nervous. I'm not keen on interrogating a guy who just had a triple bypass, but Drew thinks he might be more open with me.

He also pointed out that we'll be in the hospital if something happens, and the doctors are only a few feet away. Sarcasm much?

The only reason I agree to visit Conrad again is I think there's an excellent chance that he's our killer - now that we've discovered Simon was in jail at the time of the murder. Why can't he just admit it, so I don't have to go to the trouble of coaxing it out of him?

I bring flowers with me to the hospital. I suppose it seems lame, but how could I show up empty-handed?

It helpful that the owner of the Roses Are Red Flower Shop next door knew Gran and gives us gorgeous floral arrangements to display at the cafe. Not surprisingly, the rabbits love her because she often has fresh flowers for them to eat. In honor of Snickers' visit, she gave them roses, and those were a big hit.

"Hey there, killer!" Conrad laughs as I visibly cringe. "Oh, come on, if I can laugh about it, you can too."

"How are you feeling today?" I ask.

"I'll be a lot better if you're hiding a cocktail in them flowers, little lady!" he bellows.

"I'm sorry, I didn't think to bring a cocktail. I also want to apologize if my pestering you about Doyle's killer caused you any distress. I feel responsible," I admit.

"Nah, the doctors have been at me for years to exercise and eat better. But what do they know, right?"

I try to smile at his joke, but considering he's lying in a hospital bed, following a heart attack and triple bypass, the doctors might know a thing or two. "I don't want to upset you again, but here's the thing. We called your friend at the Morrison Group, and he said you canceled at the last minute."

"Ah, yes, I admit, I didn't have a chance to call him before you did and tell him to lie for me, now, did I?" He laughs again. He seems to be enjoying his hospital stay. They must have him on a lot of painkillers.

Plus, I can't believe he openly admits to lying about his alibi.

"You really want to know?" he asks with a tease in his voice.

"Yes, please."

"In Gunnison, fulfilling the requirements of my court-ordered community service," he sighs.

"Your what?"

He throws his hands in the air. "Do I have to spell this out for you?"

"That would be helpful." I still don't know where he's going with this.

"I got a DUI on New Year's Eve, and as part of my plea deal, I had to do 100 hours of community service."

"I'm confused."

"I was picking up trash on the side of the road, okay? Have your boyfriend check the records or call my probation officer. Call her right now. I promise she'll confirm my whereabouts."

He's shouting again, and it makes me nervous. The last thing I need is another heart attack on my conscience.

"This makes little sense. Instead of admitting you had a DUI, you'd rather I suspect you of murder?" Now I'm the one getting agitated.

"Of course! I *know* I didn't kill Max Doyle, appealing as it may have seemed sometimes, and I knew I could prove it if I had to. I also know I got a DUI, and I didn't want the entire world to know if I could help it. I hedged my bets, hoping it would all pass by."

"Forgive me, but considering you lied during our last encounter, I'd like to follow up on this alibi right here." It's ridiculous that he'd rather be suspected of murder than have everyone find out he had a DUI, and I'm totally calling his bluff. We'll see who's telling stories this time.

"No problem, little lady." He reaches for his phone on the table beside him. He holds up the phone to show me her name and number, which I dial immediately.

"Gunnison County Probation Department, this is Betty."

"Hi Betty, my name is Charlotte Duffin, and I'm here with Conrad Hanson--"

"—Hi, Betty!" he shouts.

"Yes! How's he doing?" she asks.

"Uh, well, he seems to be doing better. He's requesting cocktails."

"That sounds like him." She giggles.

What a salesman. He's even charmed his probation officer.

"This may seem like a strange question, but I'd like to confirm that he was in Gunnison performing community service over the 4th of July weekend."

"He sure was!"

Drat. There goes another one.

"Okay, thank you for your time," I tell her and hang up. Now what?

"Satisfied?" he asks a smug look on his face that kind of makes me want to smack him. I needed him to be the killer.

I try to smile, but it isn't sincere. I'm getting nowhere on this case, and time is running out.

"I appreciate your time again, and I'm happy to see you're getting better," I tell him.

"No problem! See you around, little lady!"

On the way back to Marcall's, I text Drew and ask him to confirm Doyle's arrest over the New Year's holiday. Just to be extra certain.

He writes back and tells me that yes, there is a record of Conrad's arrest and that he personally knows the probation officer. So, Conrad is telling the truth. He got arrested for a DUI on New Year's Eve but then used his money and influence to get off with nothing more than community service.

What's that joke about not wanting to know how they make the sausage? I've come across so much corruption and influence-peddling since I started investigating this, it boggles my mind.

At the last minute, I remember I wanted to follow up on my conversation with Nan, so I let Damien know that I'll make a quick detour to the elementary school library.

The serene library I expected turned out to be mostly chaos. There are a lot of kids here. Some quietly read in a corner while others shout at a video game on a computer. Another group appears to be working on a craft project and making a mess.

The sign over the doorway reads "Harriet Pointer Library" and underneath it is a quote, *There is more treasure in books than in all the pirate's loot on Treasure Island.*

"Hi there, Nan!"

"Can I help you?" she asks.

"I'm the owner of Marcall's; where you had your breakfast meeting yesterday?"

"Oh! Yes! Of course. I'm so sorry. It's been chaotic here today. I knew you looked familiar."

"If you don't mind, I wanted to follow up with you on what you told me about Mayor Doyle, but you left before I got the chance."

"You're supposed to whisper in the library!" a little girl with a carefully pressed sundress and starched ribbons in her hair, waiting to check her books out, reminds me with a finger to her lips.

"You're right. I should whisper," I tell her, trying not to sound too sarcastic.

Nan rolls her eyes at me. "Future school principal," she whispers.

"Were you in town last weekend?" I whisper back at her. The urge to turn and stick my tongue out at the little girl is strong. Doesn't she know she's supposed to respect her elders?

"I was in Vail at a conference on school library management."

"They had a conference over the 4th of July weekend?" I ask.

"The conference ended before that, but I decided to stay the entire weekend. The hotel offered a good deal because summer is their slowest time. I decided on a spur-of-the-moment to enjoy a mini-vacation."

"Oh, that's nice." I nod my head. That's disappointing. I was hoping she wouldn't have an alibi, of course.

"Miss Nan!" a boy shouts. Why doesn't that little girl yell at him for not whispering? "Billy just spilled juice all over the encyclopedias!"

Nan drops her head in her hands. "You see why we needed that mobile library?" she moans. "How am I going to get the juice out of those books?"

"If you don't mind, I could give it a shot."

She seems confused at first, but then it dawns on her. "Oh, yeah, go ahead! It would help me a lot."

I nod my head. "Sure," I tell her.

I walk over to the shouting boy, and sure enough. They've spilled an entire foil package of juice on several books, and it's already soaking in.

I whisper a simple directive over the mess, and the juice quickly dries up and disappears. The boys stare at me wide-eyed.

I can imagine what their dinner table conversation will sound like tonight. "You know that lady who tried to kill Conrad Hanson? She cleaned up our juice mess in the library with magic!"

Okay, so the kids probably don't know who Conrad Hanson is, but that's still how I picture it.

When I look for Nan again, she's deep in conversation with a group of young girls who appear to be fighting over a beanbag. I guess I'll see myself out.

Chapter 19

That afternoon I'm watching the news on the small tv I keep in Marcall's in the event there's breaking news. Or I just want to catch up on one of my favorite reality tv shows.

"An anonymous source has come forward with shocking footage of the night Mayor Doyle was stabbed to death in front of the Thai One On Food Truck..."

I have a bad feeling about this.

"The knife used to stab Mayor Doyle came from the food truck in question. Despite maintaining his innocence, Sam Bunmi, the truck's owner, was arrested earlier this week on suspicion of murdering the mayor."

Then they show footage of the cringe-worthy fight between Mayor Doyle and Mr. Bunmi, in addition to the video of him being led away in handcuffs.

"Okay, so tell me something I don't know," I mutter angrily at the television.

"A witness came forward with a video recording of Mr. Bunmi walking through the park at midnight on the night in question. Roughly the same time, Mayor Doyle was murdered."

Oh, dear. I was kidding when I said I wanted to see something new. This gets worse by the moment. Aranya's mom insisted he was home all night.

But he obviously couldn't be in two places at once. The camera then cuts to Aranya as reporters call out questions.

"No comment!" she scowls at them hurrying away.

"You tell em' Aranya!" I shout at the tv just as Aranya happens to walk into the cafe in person. I quickly turn it off, but it's too late. She saw me watching the coverage.

"You've seen it." She hangs her head.

"What's the deal with the video? It's a mistake, right? Your mom said he was home the entire night."

Aranya bursts into tears. "After this came out, my mom admitted she woke up around midnight because of the noisy fireworks some kids were setting off. Then she realized my dad was missing."

I gasp. "Oh, that's bad," I tell her.

"You think?" she sniffles. She's still unhappy with me, and I don't blame her.

"How does your dad explain that?" I ask.

"I haven't had a chance to ask him yet because they restricted his visiting hours."

"Okay, well, when you can, you'll ask him. I assume that there's a logical explanation for it."

"I'm sure there is, but this is scary."

Then she gets a text message and gapes at her phone as a fresh round of tears ensues. "Oh, no!" she cries.

"What is it?"

"They're taking the food truck right now!"

"I thought you said your parents had 48 hours!" I exclaim. "It's only been a day! How can they do that?"

"I don't know!" she screams in near hysteria. "But they're taking it now!"

She shoves her phone in my face and I watch in horror as the news shows the Thai One On food truck being towed away with a giant red sign on the door reading PROPERTY OF CRESTED PEAKS CREDIT UNION.

I am the worst friend in the world. Aranya counted on me to help her family, and I failed her.

Chapter 20

I realize I need a break from all the turmoil. I may not be interested in camping alone as Simon suggested. Or camping at all really. But sometimes, I enjoy puttering around in a rowboat that the Hotel Glacier rents out to guests to use on the lake behind the hotel. I think it's relaxing, and it's a cool summer evening with a soft breeze, so it's a perfect way to clear my head.

"Don't forget your oars!" the man who rents the boats calls out to me.

"Oh, I'm good!" I assure him as I magic the boat forward. I suppose I could row the boat the traditional way, but tonight I just want to sit and think.

When Harvey appears on the bow seat across from me, I almost scream I'm so startled.

"Good evening, lovely lady!"

"Harvey, you nearly scared me to death!" I exclaim, clutching at my chest to slow down my racing heart.

"Scared you to death!" he chuckles. "That's a good one." Then he tilts his transparent head at me. "What's troubling you, my friend?"

Harvey has been with the Hotel Glacier since the late 1800s. Yes, Harvey is a ghost. Killed in a shootout between the sheriff and a bank robber, but so busy with his job as the hotel manager that he never went into the light. Like many other interesting people in this town, he's been a font of information when I need help with a case.

"I really blew it, Harvey. Aranya trusted me to find the mayor's killer and get her dad out of prison. Even Drew asked me to help investigate, but now the Bunmi's have lost their food truck, and an innocent man is still in jail, and I'm nowhere near finding the killer."

"You have your standard list of suspects, I presume?"

"I do."

"Want to share?"

"Conrad Hanson and Simon Pointer were the most obvious. At least that's what I thought."

He nods slowly. "I could see why you'd suspect them. They were enemies of the mayor."

"Exactly. But they both have solid alibis."

"So, who's next?"

I shrug. "I keep going back to Nan Leblanc, but she insists she was in Vail at a conference when the mayor was killed, and while I know she despises him, I'm not sure it's enough motive for murder."

"Nan Leblanc, the librarian at the elementary school?"

"Yeah. You know her?"

"Odd you mention her. I saw her here recently with the now-deceased mayor. They ate dinner together."

"Perhaps they were meeting about the mobile library?"

"It could be. You undoubtedly know more than I. But it sticks out in my mind because she got very angry in the middle of dinner, threw a drink in his face, shouted, 'I'm not that kind of girl!' and then stormed out. I suspect he - how do you kids say it - hit on her?"

"Do you think he harassed her? What if he made funding the mobile library conditional on dating him?"

"I would bet on it. He acted horribly embarrassed. Which he should have been. Everyone in the restaurant stared and pointed at him. In my experience, and believe me, I've had much life experience as a ghost; it appeared like some creepy old fella hitting on a pretty young lady.

"Harvey, if I could, I would hug you. You may have blown another case wide open," I tell him.

"Aw shucks, m'lady, twas nothing," Harvey responds.

If I didn't know any better, I would say he's blushing. Can ghosts blush?

I quickly finish up my rowing session. I need to check on Nan's alibi, and if I find out she's lying too, I'm going straight to Drew with it.

This time, I won't tell Aranya until they arrest someone else. Failing to fund a mobile library may not be enough to push someone to murder but tying that funding to special favors could be. Didn't I tell Miles earlier that I think she could have accidentally killed him?

Chapter 21

When I arrive home, the rabbits rush me at the door. "Hey, lady!" Marcus and Marshall shout. "We think Snickers discovered something."

Uh oh. What now?

"There's no body in the backyard or anything, is there?" I ask, almost afraid to hear the answer.

Marshall and Marcus laugh. Because a dead body is hilarious.

"No, silly, but Snickers overheard a conversation in the alley behind the smoothie bar today."

"Why were you in the alley behind the smoothie bar?"

"We were helping ourselves to the fluffy carrot tops they store for composting."

"Ah, okay."

"We keep trying to persuade them to set the tops aside for us, but they can't hear us. Have you ever tried them? They're delicious!"

"I've never tried them, but I'll keep it in mind."

They stare back at me.

"I thought you had something to tell me?"

"Oh, yeah!" they put their heads together and giggle.

"Snickers overheard two men in the alley talking about how some guy named Simon better pay up if he wants to keep his mom out of jail. Didn't you say one of your suspects is named Simon?" Marshall asks.

"Yes! Well, he was a suspect. Now I'm not so sure. He has a rock-solid alibi. But why would he need to keep his mom out of jail? Are we sure it's the same, Simon?" Although, given the sketchy duo who showed up at his office, and his arrest for threatening the casino security guards, I bet they're connected.

"Okay, never mind then," Marcus says as they start to hop away.

"Well, wait. Tell me what he heard, anyway. Or is that all he heard?"

The two of them confer with Snickers again.

"One of them said they used their phone to film Simon's mom at a fight," Marshall explains.

"A fight? What fight?" Just as I think these three are pulling my leg, I remember how the crowd filmed the fight at the park on the 4th of

July and how much it annoyed me. "Wait, the fight between Aranya's dad and the mayor?" I ask.

Marshall shrugs. "Snickers says that's all he heard. We drowned out the rest of the conversation with our loud chewing."

"That's good, right? Good, that we overheard that?" Marcus asks.

I don't know what this means, but my gut tells me it's important. "Um, yeah, you did a good job," I respond distractedly, my mind whirring like crazy.

"So, we get treatos, right?"

"Oh, of course."

"When?" Marshall demands.

These rabbits and their treats. "I bought some cherries today. How about a piece of cherry?"

"Yay!" the rabbits jump up and down, cheering.

After I give them each a slice of cherry and Stumpy a piece of chicken because he always has to be in on it, of course, they run off, and I sit down to think. Are those two creeps blackmailing Simon because they filmed his mom at the fight on the 4th of July?

Even though she should have been in the hospital? In that case she's obviously not catatonic like Simon claimed. Does Nan still have a role in all of this?

I'm convinced somehow, she does. Why didn't she mention that she was mad enough at the mayor to throw a drink in his face? So many questions, not enough answers.

Chapter 22

I pace the floor most of the night, only pausing to take notes here and there when I don't want to forget an important detail. The rabbits watch and occasionally throw out suggestions.

However, most of them involve ways to get more parsley. Stumpy went to bed hours ago. He assumes the rabbits have this handled.

What I know so far is that Simon and Conrad have solid alibis confirmed by law enforcement. But with Nan, she happily told me how much she hated Doyle, yet conveniently left out the part where she threw a drink in his face. In front of a restaurant full of people.

Then there's this alleged video the creeps have of Harriet Pointer. Assuming that's who they were talking about, which given the family history, I have every reason to believe it is her. Was she in the crowd at the fight and they filmed her? In all the chaos, she may have blended in. Still so many questions.

Yet there's one thing I know for certain. I should have demanded to know more about Simon's mom. Conrad's heart attack spooked me, which made me afraid to push any boundaries with Simon.

Then I felt self-conscious with everyone gossiping about me giving Conrad a heart attack. I should have ignored them all and gone with my instincts. Who cares what people think?

When I realize what time it is, I'm shocked to discover I've been going over this all night and if I don't hurry, I'll be late for work. I take a quick shower, though, and just as I tell the boys we have to hurry, I see Snickers chewing on something.

"What do you have, boy?" I bend down to inspect it to ensure it isn't something important. Rabbits love their treats, but they also love to chew on cardboard and paper.

"It fell out of your purse when you got home last night," Marshall says.

"We told him he could have it," Marcus adds.

"What is it?" I ask.

It turns out it's a bookmark I picked up from the library yesterday. They had a stack of them at the doorway with a sign that said "free." I'm constantly losing my bookmarks and often have to resort to a sticky note or gum wrapper to mark my place, so I grabbed a few.

These bookmarks have the library hours, contact information, and suggestions for summer reading. But my breath catches in my throat when I see the library's name. Again. I saw it yesterday, but with all the unexpected chaos and noise, it didn't register at the time.

Harriet Pointer Library. Mrs. Pointer must have donated money to the school for the library, so they named it after her. So, wouldn't Nan know her? I hand the bookmark back to Snickers.

"Let's go, boys!" I shout. "Today will be a busy day!"

Chapter 23

During the mid-morning lull at the cafe, Damien finally asks. "All right. What's up? I know you well enough by now to realize something is afoot."

"I promise I'll let you and everybody else know as soon as I check out one more thing. Now that it's quiet, I need you to mind the shop while I run to the library."

"You swear you'll fill me in the moment you get back?"

"Don't I always?"

I walk so quickly to the library that people on the sidewalk jump out of my way. Sorry everyone, but this is essential business - there isn't a moment to spare.

When I arrive, I'm relieved to see Miles. If Nan attended the library management conference in Vail, Miles must have been there too, right? I cross my fingers and hope for the best.

"Miles!" I exclaim so loudly that he nearly jumps out of his seat. Meanwhile, several readers glare at me for interrupting their quiet. Good thing they aren't that little girl from the school library.

"Inside voices!" he laughs with a finger against his lips.

"Sorry!" I drop my voice to a whisper. "I have something important to ask you, and I forgot for a moment that we're in the library."

"What's up?"

"Were you at the library management conference last week in Vail?"

"Nah, I hate those things," he says, shaking his head.

Rats. I thought surely, he'd be there.

"I sent Stacey instead."

"Stacey?"

"She's our circulation manager."

"Yes!" I pump my fist in the air, and several people again glare at me.

"Do I have to throw you out?" he asks teasingly. "What has you so wound up?"

"Tell me Stacey is here today," I plead.

"She is. I just saw her. I'll walk you to her office. In the meantime, keep it down to a dull roar, okay?"

While we walk to her office, he asks. "Are you going to tell me what you're so excited about, or is this a secret?"

"I'll share when I know more for certain."

"Or I can just get it from Miranda?" he asks.

"That too," I admit.

"Hey Stacey, this is my good friend Charlotte. She owns Marcall's Breakfast Cafe across from Miranda's coffee shop."

"Marcall's? I love that place!" she exclaims. "But I've always wanted to ask. Why the name Marcall's?"

"My grandma's rabbit familiars are Marshall and Marcus, so it's a combination of their names."

"Ohhhh, like their celebrity name."

"Yes!" I exclaim.

"That's so cute. I love it. But what can I do for you two?"

Miles holds his hand out in my direction. "It's your question, Charlotte."

"Miles tells me you were at the library management conference in Vail last week."

"Yes!"

"I don't suppose you know Nan Leblanc, the librarian at the elementary school?"

"Of course, I know her! She's a good friend. We had cocktails together the first night of the conference."

"Do you know if she stayed there over the weekend?" I cross my fingers behind my back. If she doesn't know, I'm at a loss. I already called the hotel, but they said those records are confidential and wouldn't tell me if or when she checked out of the hotel.

"I know for a fact that she didn't stay for the weekend. I saw her leave early. I don't know why, but she ran out in a hurry. I worried that something went wrong, but she seemed fine when I saw her the other day."

"I knew it!" I shout again. This time, several people actively shush me. I have got to control myself. "Thank you!" I exclaim, but still a little too loudly. I hug Miles, who is thoroughly confused. Worried I'll shout again. I point at Stacey. "Your next breakfast is on the house!"

She's also surprised and confused but pleased at the thought of a free breakfast.

"Oh, one more thing," I pause, holding my finger in the air, "weird question, but do you know why Nan threw a drink at the mayor when they had dinner?"

She doesn't answer, but her face says everything. Mayor Doyle changed his mind about the mobile library because Nan wouldn't date him.

"I'll see you later!" I tell Miles as I turn to leave.

"Wait!" he hisses, grabbing my arm to keep me from leaving. "You aren't still thinking Nan is a suspect, are you? There's no way."

Stacy's expression tells me she heard the question, but I doubt she understands what it means.

"I don't know for certain, but the clues are falling into place, and it's bad for her," I whisper back.

With that, I scurry toward the door. There's still a lot of work to do.

I stop in the entryway when I remember to call Drew and ask him if he can get into the hospital where Harriet Pointer is. If Simon told the truth and they didn't allow anyone but him to see her, I think it will require a visit from law enforcement. If he lied, then, well, it should still have more impact with a visit from him.

While I wait for Drew to answer the phone, I peruse some pictures on the wall. Snapshots on a bulletin board with the title *Memories*.

The photos show people enjoying activities in the library. There's a cute one of a little boy reading to a golden retriever who has his head in the boy's lap.

There's another with Miles and the entire library staff. "C'mon, Drew, pick up." This time I say it softly, so no one else gets mad.

There's a picture of the Easter bunny passing out books to kids. I groan in frustration when Drew's voicemail answers for him.

"Hey, it's me. I need you to--" I stop short when I spot a picture that answers one more question.

"I knew it!" I shout, ripping the picture off the wall. Then I spot a librarian marching toward me, and she's not happy. Oops. "Drew! Call me! Now!" I add when I remember I'm still in the middle of a voice mail.

Then - I still can't believe I'm doing this; I'm stealing from the library - "I'm so sorry!" I yell back to the librarian as I dash down the steps, sprinting down Main Street.

Chapter 24

I wonder what the penalty is for stealing from the library. It's not like it's a book or anything. I'll bring it back, so really, I'm just borrowing. Which is what a library is for anyway, right?

After I run an entire block, I glance behind me to make sure the librarian isn't chasing me before I pause to text Drew with instructions on what I need him to do next. Hopefully, I haven't already freaked him out too badly.

Then I text Aranya and Miranda and tell them to meet me at the cafe immediately. One more glance over my shoulder to make sure I'm not being followed, and I head back to Marcall's. I'm getting that food truck back and freeing Mr. Bunmi if it's the last thing I do.

The three of us arrive at the cafe at almost the same time, surprising Damien when we walk in together.

"Oh dear, why does this make me nervous?" he asks.

"I'm just as in the dark as you," Miranda says.

"I'm not sure why I'm here either," Aranya responds with skepticism. "I have a lot to do today. Like try to keep my family together."

I take a deep breath. "Aranya, I owe you a huge apology. The other day, I should have been more forthcoming with you. I wanted to make you feel better, and instead, I only led you on.

"I didn't lie; I really thought that Simon killed the mayor and that it would all be over soon. But I didn't know that for sure, and I should have been clearer about that."

Aranya visibly relaxes. "I know you didn't mean to hurt my family. I should have asked you more questions about what happened. I needed to believe it would be over soon, so I may have just heard what I wanted to hear."

I continue, nodding my head. "I realize now that I should have been more confident about following up with certain leads. But I let Conrad's heart attack spook me. I got the yips, as they say."

"It's okay. I shouldn't have put this entire burden on you." Aranya hugs me.

"You were scared about what could happen to your family, and with good reason. I can't imagine what I'd do if they wrongly accused someone I loved.

"I hated it when they accused me. I felt so helpless. But the important thing now is that we catch the real killer and get your family's truck back."

"How are we going to do that?" Aranya asks.

"I'm glad you asked. I have good reason to believe that Harriet Pointer, Simon's mom, and Nan Leblanc are somehow involved in Mayor Doyle's death."

"What?" Damien exclaims in shock.

"The first time I talked to Simon, I kept thinking I should interview his mother, but with her hospitalized, I worried about making her worse, and because of what happened with Conrad, I let it slide."

"What specifically makes you think they had something to do with Doyle's death?" Miranda asks.

"Snickers overheard two men talking about getting Simon to pay for a video they have of his mother at a fight."

"The fight between my dad and the mayor, right?" Aranya asks, her excitement visibly growing. "Is that what you're talking about?"

I nod my head. "That's my working theory. I discovered just now, thanks to Miles, that Nan Leblanc lied to me about being in Vail when the mayor was killed. And--"

"There's more?" Aranya asks in shock.

I thrust the picture I just stole, er borrowed, at them. "Photographic proof." I smile proudly.

It's a picture of Nan and Harriet with their arms around each other. The caption reads: *Nan Leblanc and Harriet Pointer at the grand opening of the Harriet Pointer Library in Crested Peaks Elementary.*

They all lean in to examine the photograph, and Aranya smiles. "I told you, you could do this."

Chapter 25

"What happens next?" Damien asks. "Please tell me you aren't planning anything dangerous."

"I contacted Drew, and according to this," I hold up my phone so they can see his response to me, "he's on his way to the hospital to interview Harriet Pointer right now.

"If my hunch is correct, he'll discover that she is not catatonic and got caught unexpectedly on video from someone's phone at the fight on the 4th of July." All three of their mouths drop open. "If it's true, he'll take her into custody for further questioning."

When my phone rings and I see that it's Drew, I shoosh everybody, and the cafe goes silent.

"Hey Drew, we're ready for the good news! Lay it on us. Has Harriet confessed?"

"I don't have good news."

"You're kidding! Is Harriet pretending to be catatonic? Because you shouldn't believe that for a second! We have video proof!

"Or someone has video proof. I just know it! Can't you take her to the police station and force a confession?" The words tumble out of my mouth in a panic.

"Charlotte, let me finish. She isn't here."

"She what?" I shriek.

"She isn't here. She left. When the nurse brought her breakfast this morning, she knocked him over the head, tied him up, and stole his keys. Then she snuck out and stole a hospital van.

"They don't know where she is. I'm on my way to you. Stay put!" Drew demands. Like he thinks I'd just take off on my own or something. Although that's absolutely what I'll do.

I stare at my friends. "Harriet Pointer is gone."

Chapter 26

"She left the hospital this morning, and Drew is on his way here," I announce to my stunned friends. "He says they don't know where she is. I wonder if she went to her son's place?" I ponder out loud. "Does anyone know where he lives?"

"Boss, don't even think about it!" Damien begs.

"He lives in Pinewood Villages," Aranya tells me, much to Damien's dismay. "They have food delivered there all the time," she shrugs when we all stare at her questioningly. "874 Ponderosa Ct," she adds before Damien can stop her.

"Great! You wait here for Drew. I'll make a quick trip to his house to see if I can learn anything."

"Charlotte Duffin, don't move a muscle. You stay right here!" Damien insists. When that doesn't work. "I demand you get back here! Right this instant!" he shouts at my retreating back.

"Make me!" I yell over my shoulder.

Of course, he won't. I think he's a little afraid of me. It's not like I would hex him or anything. At least not very hard.

When I arrive at Simon's house, I jump out of my car and race for the front door, where I pound on it several times with one hand while repeatedly mashing the doorbell with the other. "Simon! Harriet! I know you're in there!" I shout.

The little voice in my head tells me this probably isn't very smart or safe, but what if they're planning to flee the country on a private jet? Mr. Bunmi could go to prison for murder, and I would always know I could have stopped it.

I continue to ring the doorbell and call out their names, to no avail. I peek in the front window to see if anyone is there, when a neighbor approaches.

"They aren't there!" she shouts. Thanks, Captain Obvious.

"I don't suppose you know where they went?" I ask.

"Beats me," she shrugs. "They often go to the family cabin when they want to get away from it all. It's one of the few things the feds didn't seize."

"Do you know where this cabin is?" I ask.

"I think I still have the directions somewhere. Hang on a sec."

The neighbor disappears into her home, and after what seems like forever, she returns with a piece of paper she hands me.

"It's not very far from here," she explains.

"Thank you so much!" I tell her. "Could you do me a huge favor? If my friends or the police come by, tell them where the cabin is too!"

"Are the Pointers in trouble again?" she asks.

"I'm not sure yet!" I shout, running back to my car.

Chapter 27

Thankfully, the cabin is easy to find, and when I get there, I see several cars parked beside it. That's odd. Why are there so many cars? I have a bad feeling about this and seriously consider calling the CPPD. But the last time I failed to follow up, it cost me.

If I had listened to my first instincts regarding Simon's mom, we wouldn't be in this mess right now. I park at the cabin next door, hoping they don't hear me. That's the best thing about the Prius. I can sneak up on almost anyone.

I tiptoe up to the side window of the cabin and peek in. Too bad there's no invisibility spell. Think of the tricks I could play on people! The first thing I see are the two greasy men from Simon's office. I knew it. I just knew it. They're the blackmailers.

Then I see Simon and Harriet each tied to a chair. I "eep" out loud I'm so surprised, and when one of the men turns to the window and asks, "What was that?" I slap my hand over my mouth.

"Dude, it was nothing. Just a cat probably," the other guy says.

"I suppose," the man responds.

That was close. I continue scanning the room, but I wish I had a clearer view of what's happening. One of them has moved into my line of sight, and now I can't see Simon or Harriet.

I have to call the police. I pull my phone from my pocket, but before I can dial, someone grabs me from behind, knocking my phone to the ground.

Chapter 28

I scream and kick and search for something big to smack him over the head. Then in a burst of brilliance, and possibly even stupidity, I decide I want to get inside the cabin.

I must know the truth, and if I knock this guy out with the lawn chair I just saw and run away, I may never know for sure. For now, I'll go along with whatever they want, and if it seems like I'm genuinely in danger, I'll use witchcraft to subdue them. If Drew ever finds out I did this, he may actually kill me for taking such a colossal risk.

I let the man drag me inside the cabin as I continue to kick and scream because I don't want him to know I'm willing to go along nicely. For now, anyway.

"What the...?" Simon exclaims when he sees me. If this were any other situation, the expression on his face would be hilarious.

"Who is that?" Harriet asks.

"Yeah, who is that Mo?" the guy who didn't just kidnap me asks.

"She showed up to my office the other day asking questions about dad and everything that happened with Max," Simon explains to his mom.

"Why?" Harriet asks.

"Supposedly, it's something about one of her employees. Her dad is Bunmi, the guy who's in jail for killing Max."

"You obviously lied about your mother being catatonic and not recognizing you!" I grumble.

"You told her I was catatonic?" Harriet asks. "Why did you tell her that?"

"I thought she was a reporter!" Simons whimpers.

"Wait. I'm in charge here. Why were you creeping around outside?" Mo asks.

"I dropped my car keys?"

"Oh, you're hilarious."

"Hey, I recognize her! He's right," he gestures to Simon. "She's the chick from his office the other day."

"Whatever. Help me tie her up, Larry," Mo insists.

"Where's Curly?" I have to ask.

"Huh?" Larry says.

I shake my head. Just what I always wanted. I'm being held hostage by a pair of morons.

They shove me down onto a chair and tie my hands behind me.

"You better not be blackmailing him, too," Mo warns. "We were here first! Did you know he told *us* that his old lady didn't recognize him?"

I laugh because I can't help it. "I'm not blackmailing him, but I have to know. What kind of video do you have on her?" I point my head toward Harriet.

"How did you know we have video?" Larry demands.

"I told you not to tell the cops!" Mo shouts, punching Simon in the face and knocking his chair over.

"He didn't tell me!" I insist. "I swear."

"Then how do you know about the video?"

The only thing I can think of at this point is the truth. "My rabbits overheard you talking."

"What?" Mo exclaims. I just hope he doesn't slug me too.

"Dude! I told you I thought those rabbits were listening to us! The littlest one kept staring at me. So creepy."

Way to go, Snickers, I think to myself.

"C'mon, humor me. I swear I'm not the cops, and I'm not here for money. What is on the video?" I assume Harriet and Simon will never tell me, so I have to rely on a pair of dumb criminals to do it.

Plus, I'm stalling for time here. Drew and the CPPD will go to Simon's house, and the neighbor will direct them here. Of course, I'll get in big trouble for doing this, but I'll just deal with that when it's all over. If I can keep them talking, we're safe.

"Just tell her." Larry waves his hand. "We're going to kill them anyways."

Gulp.

"I was recording that crazy fight at Snowball Park on my phone. Just for kicks, you know. Then, when I watched it back later, I saw Simon's old lady in the background, so I decided to blackmail him. It worked!"

"Wait, you didn't even do it on purpose?" Simon bellows.

"No man, total happy accident," he laughs.

Simon is still lying on the ground, tied to the chair, while he struggles against the ropes, hoping to untie himself.

I turn to Harriet. "I'm still missing something here. Why were you in Snowball Park on 4th of July when you were supposed to be in the hospital?"

"You don't have to tell her anything, mom," Simon urges.

"Oh, I don't care who knows anymore," Harriet responds. "But while we're all playing true confessions here, why were you telling people I was unresponsive in the hospital? You know, it's more of an exclusive spa than a hospital," she explains.

"It's more like a hospital for the super-rich when they need to hide from reporters and cops. How's that?" Simon retorts.

"Whatever." Harriet rolls her eyes.

"If you must know, when they showed me the video, I worried that you killed Max, so I thought if I told them you were off your rocker and unable to speak or recognize anybody, they'd back off," Simon explains. "I didn't realize that set me up to be blackmailed."

And even I fell for it, I realize.

"Hang on a second," Larry says. "So, you weren't ever catatonic, and you didn't kill the mayor?"

Harriet snorts. "I was never catatonic, as you say, but I'm kind of impressed my son thought of that story, even if he did mess it up in the end, and yes, I did kill Mayor Doyle."

Chapter 29

"You what?" Mo, Larry, and I all exclaim in stereo.

"It's all that foolish Nan's fault. She had this so-called brilliant idea to hire a pair of thugs to beat up Max for everything he did to us."

I stare at the goons. "Don't look at us!" Larry exclaims.

"No, it wasn't them. It was someone else, you dimwit." Harriet snaps at me.

"Oh. Sorry." I tell them as they both shrug.

"I could see where you might think that." Larry nods his head.

"Anyway!" Harriet grunts. I guess she doesn't like me stealing the spotlight. I'm still just stalling for time. "I went along with it because why not? Nan picked me up that morning from the *spa*," she emphasizes, gloating at all of us, "only they didn't show. They took her money and ran. I told her never to pay upfront, but of course, she wouldn't listen to me."

"But how did she convince Mayor Doyle to meet her at midnight?" I ask.

"He originally told Nan if she wanted a mobile library, she had to go out with him--"

"Ha!" I proclaim. Called that one. Thanks to Harvey anyway.

Harriet glares at me for interrupting again. "--But after she embarrassed him at the restaurant, he backed out of funding her project. So, in order to get him to the park that night, she told him she changed her mind about being willing to date him and that she would meet up with him."

"He fell for that?" Simon asks.

"Nothing like a foolish old man to be lured in by a pretty young thing. But even I admit, we were a little surprised that he agreed to it. Then while we were waiting for everyone to show up, I got bored and, just for kicks, turned the knob on the food truck, and it opened! I went inside, thinking they might have a bottle of water or, even better, a bottle of scotch."

Then she laughs at her own joke. "But from inside the camper I heard Nan call for help. Max, believing she'd changed her mind, tried to kiss her, and she wanted none of it. I saw the knife sitting on the counter and thought, what the heck, I'll just scare him a little--"

"Mom, stop!" Simon exclaims so sharply that the rest of us are startled.

"Shut up, man; she was just getting to the good part!" Mo yells while threatening to hit him again.

"Mom, you can't keep admitting this." Simon begs.

"We're killing all of you anyway, so we may as well hear the end of the story," Larry informs us.

"Confession is good for the soul," Mo says while I nod my head. I can't believe I'm playing along with these goons. Where is the CPPD? Where is Drew?

We're all so enthralled with listening to Harriet tell her story that we lean towards her, waiting for the exciting conclusion. The cabin is silent. But when we hear something crash outside, we all jump. My first thought is, finally, it's the cops!

Weirdly, my second thought is, but she hasn't finished her story! Larry runs out the door and I hold my breath, waiting to hear the familiar, "Freeze! Crested Peaks Police Department!" But when I don't, I'm confused. What are they doing out there? When Larry drags a struggling Nan Leblanc into the cabin, my heart sinks.

Chapter 30

"Who the heck is that?" Mo asks. "Why do people keep showing up like we're having a party here? What is wrong with this town?"

"I found her sneaking around outside!" Larry says.

"Hello Nan," Harriet sneers.

I sigh. Why did she admit to knowing her? Now they'll take her hostage as well. Not that they'd let her go, she's already seen them, and they can't have that.

Larry pushes Nan into a chair while Mo ties her up. "If I'd known people were going to keep showing up, I'd have brought more rope!" he grumbles.

"Stacey told me you were looking for me," she says.

"I wasn't really *looking* for you." I point out. "Just *asking* about you."

"How dumb are you?" Harriet complains, glaring at her.

"Knock it off, ladies!" Mo says. "I believe you were about to finish your story," he nods his head at Harriet.

"Where was I?" she asks.

"After hearing a commotion outside the food truck, you grabbed a knife," Larry reminds her.

"Ah, yes. So, he could have just run away, but oh no, he lunged at me, and then I stabbed him. It felt good! I think you could consider it kind of an accident, but I don't regret it."

"I think she's colder than we are," Mo says to Larry.

"Hardly!" I scold them. "She stabbed one guy, but you plan to kill all of us!"

"She's got us there, man." Larry nods.

Now it's my turn to ask a question. "Hang on a second, Harriet. Sam Bunmi insists that when he checked the door around midnight that it was locked. But you're saying it wasn't, and that's how you got in? How did that happen?"

"I don't know! I just know it wasn't locked when I tried it. I didn't say I had an answer for everything!" she snaps. "If you don't mind, I'd like to finish."

Simon groans and shakes his head while Larry and Mo nod theirs, egging her on.

"Nan here wanted to pull the knife out and run, but I convinced her to leave it. At the last second, I locked the door, thinking that way the police wouldn't connect the knife to the food truck. Oops." She shrugs

"All righty!" Larry interrupts, rubbing his hands together. "This was entertaining, but we have to go."

For a moment, I'm relieved. They decided not to kill us. They're just going to take off. I wonder how fast the CPPD can get here and how much of a head start the bad guys will have.

"Is it set?" he nods at Mo.

"All set!" Mo responds.

"What's set?" Simon asks.

"The explosion," Larry says.

"Explosion?" Nan cries. "What explosion?"

"We're blowing up the cabin," Mo responds, as if she should have realized that all along.

"Isn't that a bit extreme?" I ask.

"Nah," says Mo, waving his hand dismissively. "Shooting people is too messy. Besides, it gives me the creeps to watch them die in front of me."

"You're killing us because of a failed blackmail attempt?" I ask.

"Oh no, we're killing you because you idiots can identify us now, and we're killing Simon because he owes us $250,000 in gambling debt, and we're tired of waiting for him to pay up. We'll use him as a lesson to all the other deadbeats."

"$250,000?" Harriet exclaims.

"Ah ha! You are loan sharks." I point out.

"Whatever, lady," Mo says.

"How exactly are you planning to blow us up?" I ask. I need to know so I can prevent it. Thankfully, they don't know I'm a witch. Good thing they'd never believe the story about the rabbits talking to me.

"Easy peasy lemon squeezy, lady. It's an old cabin, so it will appear that the gas leak we've already set up is from the aging gas line. There will be nothing left of you and all your friends.

"All they'll find are itty bitty charred pieces, and we'll be long gone. As a bonus, if anyone is foolish enough to try to rescue you - BOOM!" He shouts, throwing his hands in the air and laughing hysterically at the way we all jump.

My mind churns. In order to save all of us and keep Drew and the CPPD from blowing up, I must untie myself and Simon and Harriet and Nan and overtake Mo and Larry before they allow the gas in, and I'm overwhelmed just thinking about it. I'm not that powerful of a witch. It's too many people to deal with all at once.

Sure, I could just save myself, and as tempting as that might seem in the moment, it wouldn't help Aranya's dad.

What if they didn't believe me when I tell them Harriet confessed to killing the mayor? Or that she and Nan set it all up to begin with?

The truth would be impossible to confirm. They might think I said that to save Mr. Bunmi, knowing that the other witnesses were all dead.

My best shot at saving all of us and getting Sam out of jail is to neutralize the gas, and even that's a tremendous undertaking.

Nan begs and pleads with them to let us go. She swears she'll claim she never saw them.

She even insists they should untie her since she was the last one there but leave everyone else tied up. What a swell person.

"You call yourself a children's librarian," I scold while she gives me an icy glare. It's true, though!

"The gas line is in the kitchen," Mo explains. "You start the car and I'll loosen the line."

Larry nods. "It's been swell folks, but I gotta go!" He waves to us as he heads out the door.

Simon, Nan, and Harriet all scream at him, begging him to let them go while Mo disappears into the kitchen, and I prepare myself to neutralize the gas somehow.

We all hear the whoosh of gas pouring out of the line in the kitchen and Nan bursts into tears. Harriet continues to curse while Simon struggles to get free of the ropes.

"See you never!" Mo calls out as he sprints through the living room, slamming the front door behind him.

Chapter 31

Simon, Nan, and Harriet are all screaming now, and I can't concentrate enough to do what I need to. "Quiet!" I snap at them. They're all so stunned they stop screaming to gawk at me. "I need to concentrate."

Simon laughs. "Why on earth would you need to *concentrate?* Concentrate on dying?"

"Wait, you guys, she's a witch!" Nan exclaims.

"I can neutralize the gas, but I need silence."

Harriet regards me skeptically, but at this point what does she have to lose? "All right. Let her work."

The gas fumes flooding the cabin are so thick I'm convinced I could reach out and grab a handful.

Tears stream down Nan's face while she tries not to panic. "I think I'm going to throw up!" she moans.

Part of me wants to remind her that if she went to the cops right away, none of us would be here right now.

"If you throw up, I'll throw up!" Simon complains.

"You fools! Let her work!" Harriet chastises them.

I breathe deep and slow, trying not to think about the fumes I'm inhaling, and concentrate instead on generating the atmosphere's cleansing powers. I call on my connection to the earth's essence and I beseech her to clear the air we're breathing and allow nature's magic to quell the toxic fumes.

At first, I worry I'm imagining it, but bit by bit the atmosphere begins to clear.

"The police are here!" Harriet cries.

"What if it still isn't safe for them to open the door?" Simons asks. "What if there's still too much gas?"

They scream at the police not to come inside, but I doubt the police can hear them. Meanwhile I continue to work at reducing the gas because every second counts. If I can clear the air just enough, it should be safe. But before I think I'm ready, Drew kicks down the door and several officers follow on his heels.

Simon, Harriet, Nan and I all scream in terror. We can't help it. We're about to be blown to...

Chapter 32

When Simon laughs with glee, I open my eyes and realize we didn't blow up. It's working.

"You did it!" Nan shouts.

Drew and the officers are momentarily stunned at the sight before them. Definitely not what they were expecting.

"I smell gas!" one shouts.

"In the kitchen!" I tell him.

"Go!" Drew barks, pointing that direction while several officers run in there to turn it off. I immediately magic my way out of the ropes and jump up from the chair before they can get the others untied.

Miranda and Damien then rush into the house despite being told to stay back. Her jaw drops when Miranda sees Harriet, Simon, and Nan tied up while I'm free.

She stares at me and back at them, then returns to me. "Why did you tie them up?"

Damien, Miranda, and I watch as the police drive away with Simon, Harriet, and Nan in custody. "I am so glad to see you guys! Thank goodness the neighbor sent you here. I got worried!"

"What neighbor?" Miranda asks.

"Simon's neighbor. The one who told you where to find me."

"We never saw a neighbor," Drew explains. "We pinged your phone."

"Oh! Hey, where is my phone?" I ask, searching my pockets when I realize it's gone.

"It's right here!" Drew explains, waving it in the air.

"Where did you find it?"

"On the ground outside the window where you were obviously sneaking around."

Oops. "In my defense, I had it out because I meant to call the police, but I guess when Mo grabbed me, I dropped it."

"In your defense?" Drew glares at me. "I told you to wait at the cafe. No, I insisted you wait at the cafe. Not chase down wanted criminals."

"Alls well, that ends well," Damien says as he and Miranda start to tiptoe away. They obviously don't want to stick around for the tongue lashing.

"Get back here, you cowards!" I yell at them while Drew continues to lecture me on letting the professionals handle these things.

Chapter 33

It's a balmy summer evening, perfect for the farmer's market, and the line in front of the Thai One On food truck is long. Everyone is thrilled they're back. Marshall, Marcus, Snickers, and Stumpy ride in the wagon while we peruse the booths.

Snickers will go back to Toronto tomorrow morning. He's a funny little guy, and we'll miss him. I'm grateful he provided the final key to solving the mayor's murder, but I'm sure his family misses him, too.

Of course, everyone stops by the wagon and gives them all treats, which is why they like to come to these things in the first place.

"So, what's the deal?" Miranda asks. "Why did you summon all of us?"

She and Damien stare at me expectantly.

"I know what it is!" Marshall shouts.

Fortunately, none of the other humans here can hear him. The rabbits are always trying to steal my thunder.

"Hey, guys! Drew shouts as he jogs toward us.

"Hey Drew!" we call out.

"Please tell me you got them!" I clasp my hands together in prayer. I swear if those two get away with trying to blow us up, I'll never get over it.

Drew nods, a big smile on his face. "They picked them up at the New Mexico border."

Phew!

"I never doubted it! Miranda says.

"With all the evidence we have on them, they're going away for a long time," Drew says confidently. "Harriet lawyered up as we expected. Nan will plead guilty to obstruction in exchange for a reduced sentence. The elementary school will need a new librarian, though."

"And a new name!" Damien offers, and we all groan. "What, I'm the only one not allowed to make cringy jokes? The rest of you do it all the time."

"Why did you summon us?" Miranda asks the second time.

I smile coyly. "You all know, there's an opening for mayor in the election this fall."

Damien gasps with delight. Miranda's eyes widen in surprise.

"I'm running for mayor!" I squeal.

Serenity nods her head. She obviously isn't surprised.

I can't tell if Drew is impressed or stunned. Or both.

"After everything we've been through this week with these corrupt public officials, I decided it's time for a change in Crested Peaks." I announce proudly.

"Yes!" Miranda shouts, jumping up and down. "You'll be great!"

"Are you going to be mayor and still run the cafe?" Damien asks. Concern etching his face.

"Why not?" I ask.

"Phew! For a second, I was worried." Poor Damien. Always cautious. Always worried.

Drew finally recovers from the shock and hugs me. "Whatever you need, I'll help! My girlfriend, the mayor." He grins at me. "Does this mean I have to call you Ms. Mayor?"

"I hadn't thought of that." I laugh. "But let's not get ahead of ourselves. I only filed the candidate paperwork yesterday."

"We have a lot of work to do. The election will be here before you know it!" Miranda says.

"It's a week after Halloween!" I exclaim.

"Oh, I hope that isn't a bad omen," Damien responds.

"You just had to say that out loud, didn't you?" Miranda says, smacking him on the arm.

She's kidding, right?

More Books by B I Skinner

Ghostly Glenwood Mysteries Paranormal Cozy Mysteries

The Case of the Haunted Hotel

The Case of the Pilfering Poltergeist

The Case of the Poached Peridot

The Case of the Gym Ghost(Pre-order)

Spooky Shanty Realty Mysteries

Afterlife in the Attic(Pre-order)

Marcall's Breakfast Cafe Paranormal Cozy Mysteries

An Eggscellent Day for Murder

24 Carrot Caper

Daggers and Donuts

Cupcakes and Corpses

A Crime of Cranberry

Peppermints & Pandemonium

Star Spangled Homicide

Blood Curdling Ballots

Sign up for my email list here

https://mailchi.mp/9ebce0da866a/email-signup-list

Visit my website

biskinnerauthor.com

Follow me on Instagram **@bethiskinner** Facebook **@biskinnerauthor**